my father
more or less

Books by Jonathan Baumbach

My Father More or Less
The Return of Service
Chez Charlotte and Emily
Babble
Reruns
What Comes Next
A Man to Conjure With
The Landscape of Nightmare

my father more or less

a novel by

Jonathan Baumbach

FICTION COLLECTIVE

First Edition

LCCN: 81-71644
ISBN: 0-914590-66-9
ISBN: 0-914590-67-7 (paper)

Published by Fiction Collective with assistance from the National Endowment for the Arts and New York State Council on the Arts.

Grateful acknowledgement is made to the Guggenheim Foundation for a grant under which much of this novel was written.

Typeset by Open Studio in Rhinebeck, N.Y., a non-profit facility for writers, artists and independent literary publishers, supported in part by grants from the New York State Council on the Arts and the National Endowment for the Arts.

For you, G.B.

Dearest Father,

You asked me recently why I maintain that I am afraid of you. As usual, I was unable to think of any answer to your question, partly for the very reason that I am afraid of you, and partly because an explanation of the grounds for this fear would mean going into far more details than I could even approximately keep in mind while talking. And if I now try to give you an answer in writing, it will be very incomplete, because, even in writing, this fear and its consequences hamper me in relation to you and because the magnitude of the subject goes far beyond the scope of my memory and power of reasoning.

—Franz Kafka

I

I had a dream the night before last in which I had already made the trip to London and had unwittingly got into a fight with my father at Customs. We had both bought souvenir penknives from an airport shop and as a joke, as what I thought was a joke, were slicing the buttons off each other's jackets. He gets angry for no apparent reason—I had done nothing he hadn't done first—and he says, Tom, I'm going to teach you a lesson you'll remember for as long as you live. I say I'm sorry, but he jabs me with the knife, ripping a fist-size hole in the side of my jacket. The knife withdraws with a rosebud of blood at its point. You've gone too far, I say, astonished at the blood. He shuffles around, taunting me with the knife, saying, Come on, come on, let's see what you're made of. Although I am angry, I mean only to defend myself, not to strike back. When he thrusts his knife at my heart—it's as if he really means to kill me—I spear him in the back of the hand, the blade sticking, snapping off at the handle. It seems not to bother him and he comes at me again, slashing the air, pricking me in the thumb, the blade of my knife lodged like a wing in the back of his hand. You shit-faced son of a bitch, he yells. His thrusts are without force, are easily defended against. At some point I notice that the front of his shirt is thick with blood. I think, How will I get back to America if the old man dies.

I keep making this trip to London in my imagination, the same trip to visit my father, sit each time at a window seat in the No Smoking section of a Pan Am 747, the plane taxiing down a runway, changing direction, stopping and starting, trapped in indecision. There is almost always an unspecified delay that prolongs itself beyond my patience. And then without further announcement, just when I think we'll never go anywhere, we tear loose from the earth. The plane ascends with heartbreaking abruptness, Kennedy Airport reducing itself to abstraction in the distance below. I am on my way, though unready for the trip, without expectation of what awaits me on the other side.

I have a copy of one of my father's novels on my lap, a book called *Interior Corrosions,* which I will make an effort to read. Oddly, I have never been able to read any of his books word for word from beginning to end, though I had tried—give me that—had pretended to read them, had carried them with me when I was younger as though they were medals earned in battle. I had never given up the idea of some day reading his books as I had never really fully given up the idea that he would one day return to our family. He left us when I was four and Kate seven, returned inexplicably when I was five and left for good two days after my sixth birthday. Since he had left forever once and returned, I saw no reason why it couldn't happen again. My mother certainly acted as if she expected him to return, talked of his absence as if he had gone to the supermarket and forgotten the way back. I assumed that he would eventually tire of whatever he was doing (I thought of him as being like Mastroianni in *La Dolce Vita*) and return to us, his faithful family. As much as five years after he had walked out, his bed, still talked of as his, remained alongside my mother's awaiting his momentary return. We are still waiting, though with smaller investment of hope than before. He has been gone twelve years, has lived in a different state for most of five and in a different country for the past two.

I mean, it was not that we never saw him after he left. It was that there was no longer any pleasure in his presence for us, that he visited seasonally like a salesman, selling his time at inflated prices. He seemed like an imposter, this visitor from another planet, this salesman of damaged goods, an inadequate stand-in for the father we had lost. I mean, he went through the motions of being our father, tried to buy us with unexpected kindnesses. Nothing we got from him lasting or satisfying, we became tougher and tougher customers, my sister and I. Kate got married when she was twenty and moved to Colorado, got divorced the following year but stayed on among the vanished bison. She would not talk to him again, she said, unless he called to apologize for twenty-one years of damage he had done her.

Although it is a No Smoking section, the conservatively dressed black man in the seat next to me lights a cigarette, takes two drags, then holds it out absent-mindedly as it burns down, the smoke crowding my space. I cough, but say nothing, brush the smoke away with the back of my hand, expect retribution to come from one of the stewardesses passing among us, taking orders for drinks.

"It's your father's opinion," said my mother, "that I make it difficult for his children to see him, but as you can see the opposite is more nearly the truth."

I had been saying I didn't know whether I wanted to go to London and I saw no reason to go if I didn't really want to.

"There's no question that you're going," she said. "You told your father that you're going and you're not changing your mind."

"Come on," I said. "Okay? He's changed his mind when it came to seeing me any number of times. Why is everything the way he wants it?"

Her answer to that was made from under the drone of the dishwasher turned on in midsentence, and I had to ask her to repeat her remark.

I had to follow her to her room to get an answer, such as it was, from the other side of a closed door. "It's important that you have some sort of relationship with your father," she said, sniffling. "I'm not defending or attacking him. I don't want to talk about it any more. Is that clear?"

When I pushed the door open—the scene plays itself in slow motion—my mother let out a small cry and lifted the blanket up over her breasts, which were in any event fully clothed.

"Don't you dare," she said or something equally inappropriate. "You don't come into this room without knocking first."

I open my eyes to glance at my watch—we've been an hour and twenty minutes in the air—read a few more lines in my father's book. *How much silence could we bear without beginning to rave, how much talk that was only silence amplified and distorted into language? Her face pressed to the window, she watched the discolorations of the leaves as if they were*... His sentences exhaust me and I close my eyes to filter the words, to sift the meaning from the sound.

A stewardess named Marlene is talking to the man next to me. She holds her smile as if it occupied her face against her will. "And what about you?" she says to me.

"I'd like a beer," I say. "What kind do you have?"

"How old are you?" she asks.

"How old do I have to be, Marlene?"

Kate had a stomachache that day. She tended to get sick whenever my father came to take us the way some kids get sick when they have to take a test in school. My mother said that I should go alone with him because she didn't have the energy to fight with Kate and she didn't want to listen to her whine.

I said if I had to I would.

She said, "I don't want to have to fight with you too."

I said, "What are you talking about? I said I would go, didn't I?"

She said, "I don't want to hear any more about it from either of you. Is that clear?"

She hurried into her room and slammed the door, an indication that she was about to fall apart and wanted to spare us witness of her humiliation. She was still shut up in her room when the doorbell announced my father's presence. No one moved to answer. I kept thinking that I would do it—I was the only one that wasn't in some room with the door closed—but it didn't seem fair that I should have to do it all the time. "Will someone answer the door please," my mother called from her room. "Tom, what are you doing?"

The bell rang a second time, and a third. I remember walking very slowly to the door, thinking they couldn't say I wasn't trying. It wasn't even that I didn't want to see him; that wasn't the reason I couldn't get myself to the door. At that time, I still looked forward to his visits. I was open to anything.

As soon as he started up the car, he said, "Tell me again why Kate's not coming with us."

I said, "Neither of us was feeling well this morning, but I wanted to come anyway."

He said, "And Kate didn't want to come?"

I said, "She had a stomachache. It's been going around, a stomach virus, half my class has been absent."

"It sounds like an epidemic to me. I'm surprised the streets weren't closed off."

"She felt bad that she couldn't go with you. It wasn't that she didn't want to go."

"Tell me something, Tom. Does your mother make it difficult for the two of you to see me?"

"She wants us to see you, Dad. She really does."

"Like the president wants to end the war in Vietnam," he said.

He parked at a meter on Hudson Street and got out of the car. It was raining and he offered me his corduroy jacket to put over my head and I said rain didn't bother me and he said take it for God's sake. I put the jacket under my arm, then I dropped it, and he said what the hell's the matter with you?

I was always dropping things, told him about dropping a bottle of gingerale on the way home from D'Agostino's and then going back to get a second one, which I dropped and broke when I was trying to open the door to our apartment. I thought he would laugh but he didn't. He had his mind on something else.

He never mentioned the object of our destination, but I knew it was to see one of his women. The building we entered had no elevator. We wallked up a narrow staircase to the sixth floor and after knocking on the door and not waiting for an answer, went into this tiny apartment that seemed like a doll's house. This is my only son, he said. The blond woman who belonged to the apartment laughed.

The apartment was hot and I asked her if she had anything to drink.

This woman, who was too skinny to be really pretty, had the emptiest refrigerator I had ever seen in a place where somebody lived.

"You'll have to settle for a glass of water," she said, "unless you want to go out and get some pop." My father said, "He drops bottles."

"Why would you want to do that?" she asked.

I said I really didn't want any water, that I never really liked New York water, didn't she have any milk or juice.

"If he doesn't want water," she said to my father, "he can't really be thirsty."

I said I don't think it's right to call someone you don't know a liar.

Later, for something real or imagined I had done to offend her, she asked us to leave. My father left me in the hall and went back.

"Look, honey," I heard him say through the closed door, "give him a chance for God's sake. He's not a bad kid."

"I'm very upset, Lukas," she said. "This is my place and I don't have to have anyone here I don't want to see. Maybe after he's gone you can come back."

My father whispered something I couldn't make out, the word "time" coming through, repeating itself.

"If you mean that," she said, "then get rid of him."

I've had the feeling for some time—it may even extend back to the day I accepted my father's invitation—that this is a final trip for me, that I'm either not going to arrive in London or not going to get back. I've always thought of dreams as prophetic, a kind of inside out warning, and the dreams I've had concerning this trip have almost all looked into the mouth of disaster. In one, a side door of the airplane would suddenly blow open and the passengers nearest to it would be sucked out into the atmosphere. A high jacker was responsible for the door coming open and I shouted at him that it made no sense what he was doing.—I want this plane, he said. I need this plane.—That's childish, I said. None of us has ever had a 747 of his own. The man, who was undefinably familiar, said he didn't want to hear the word childish again from me. He once, in fact, threw acid in the face of a classmate who called him childish.—If there's one thing I won't tolerate, he said, it's having my manhood undermanned. The pilot was ordered to jump from the plane though the hijacker, who was not completely awful, said he could use a parachute if it gave him a greater sense of security. The pilot wanted no favors, said he didn't want to be beholden to a criminal and would take his chances on free fall. I could see that he was dissembling, that he had a parachute under his flight jacket. —Okay, said the hijacker, it's your funeral. When the door was pushed open for the pilot's jump, the suction dragged us all toward the opening. The next thing I knew I was falling among clouds of parachutists, holding on to the seat in front of me. The pilot, who occupied the seat, said not to worry there wasn't anything that flew he couldn't land. What struck me most—it was the first awareness I had of it—was that pilot and hijacker had the same face.

I mean to be dispassionate, to pass out these snapshots, these sometimes moving pictures as if I had no personal stake in them. The central figure in all is that mysterious man, that master of disguise, my father. He appears and disappears, changes his job, his appearance, his personality, the conditions of his life. It is his passion never to be the same twice. My first memory of him is with a mustache, a short thick brush, though he claims he has never worn a mustache (at least not separate from a beard). The picture is there and, accurate or not, I see no way of giving it up. The first face is the businesslike father, head of the household, smoker of fat cigars. I remember him, smelling of cigars, lifting me from the crib to rub his face into mine.

The second face is really two faces or two aspects of the same face. He is clean-shaven, elegantly dressed, hair parted down the middle, a wise guy and stand-up comic, a self-made celebrity beleaguered by admirers. He has published an award-winning novel the year before and is between books, at odds with himself. I am six years old or almost six, thinking myself six in advance of that turning point. My father takes me with him to the town house apartment of his current editor, a man who has made his career, he says, out of knowing less than nothing, a man unencumbered, goes the joke, by the obligations of intelligence. I sit in the corner shyly, playing with a small rubberized plastic Godzilla, while the men talk or rather my father talks and the other man listens. Two other people come in, a man and a woman dressed like models in the windows of expensive department stores. I am introduced and complimented on being the son of my father. More people come in, mostly men, an occasional woman. My father holds forth, holds court, while the others listen respectfully. More people wander in. My father is congratulated again. "How wonderful for you," a woman says, kissing him on both cheeks.

My father disdains admiration, says all success is fraudulent, others more than some. He is in terrific form. "Your father is in terrific form," a woman says to me, an odd-looking woman in purple velvet pants.

Whatever he says, sometimes a grunt or clearing of the throat, produces laughter. "Your father is a very funny man," the woman says to me. "Are you also a funny man?"

"I'm funnier," I say. "I have to be because no one laughs."

My questioner laughs, goes back to look for my father to repeat this remark to him. When she finds him, when she is able to dislodge his attention from elsewhere, when she repeats my remark with slight variation, my father looks puzzled then laughs extravagantly. The picture that remains is of my father and the woman laughing together with exaggerated amusement.

And there's the other side of that face: suspicious, vulnerable, stern, glowering. He would fly off the handle, as my mother called it, at invisible provocations. "I won't put up with that kind of behavior any more," he would shout. "Do you hear me, Tom?" How could I not hear him? And sometimes after one of these rages he would apologize, saying that he loved me and wanted me to forgive him, tears on his face. Kate used to forgive him (I think she was afraid not to), but I refused him that satisfaction. I put my hands over my ears when he apologized, pretended not to be able to hear him. When he left home the second time, never to return, I could take some of the responsibility for his departure.

The third face, which comes in several variations, is the face of the visiting father. It sometimes comes with full beard, sometimes artistically unshaven. Sometimes the eyes seemed so far back in the skull that I had the impression that the sockets were unfilled, that the eyes had retreated beyond return. I remember thinking that the eyes had turned around to get a view of the other side. I think of the beard as a kind of mask, and the third face, the several third faces of my father, as the old man's disguise. The beard changes shape, is pointed, is rounded, covers the entire face, covers only part of it, goes to seed like an untended garden. It is as if he were trying to hit on the most impenetrable disguise. If you can't pin him down, can't say exactly how he looks, he is safe from your knowledge.

In his most recent phone call, he said he had been thinking of shaving his beard, not to be surprised if he were beardless when I saw him.

"How will I recognize you?" I asked, only parly in jest.

"I will be the only one there who can claim to be your father."

I see it this way. Or this is one of the ways I see it. I am the man's enemy and he knows it. He has made me his enemy and is aware that he has and so he must resent and fear my presence. If that's the case, and it's the only case I have, why did he invite me to London? Certainly not for the reason he offers—to get to know me better, to make up for past failures—which he would mock as clichés if I offered them to him. I acknowledge that he may feel some guilt over the way he's treated me in the past, but I doubt that that's the main reason for his invitation. There's evidence for a completely different interpretation of his motives. The natural hostility of sons and fathers is the central theme of his novels, a friend of my mother's once told me, thinking the idea would amuse me. Let's take the argument where it goes, okay? It's dangerous not to know where your enemy is at all times. So he brings me to London to have me where he can see me, to have me in his sights. What follows? He converts me if he can to his view of things, tries to pacify my resentment. And if he can't—the reasoning seems extreme, is meant to be extreme—he gets me out of his way. The idea seems inhuman, perhaps crazy, and I neither believe it nor disbelieve it. I see it merely as one possibility on a spectrum of possibilities.

I am susceptible to motion sickness, have always been, my mother says, and on long car trips usually have to ask the driver to stop and let me out. When the sickness doesn't come its absence is itself cause for wonder. An hour and fifty-five minutes have passed on this flight and I've had a beer, dozed, read a half-page of my father's first or second novel, and I'm still all right. Queasiness, or maybe only expectation of, rises and subsides. I open the book in my lap at random and read whatever the eye chances to record.

On the other side of the closed window, in the dusty courtyard where rough gravel gathers into heaps, the truck has its hood turned toward the house. There were a few people around as there always were, no matter the hour, at the gate along which the road, connecting with the Skyline Highway, ran. I understood the signification of their continued presence, like mysterious plants that spring out of the soil, though found it without weight or interest, a familiar and ominous landscape belonging to itself.

Someone said (I forgot where I read it) that my father writes mystery stories in which there are neither corpses nor murderers, in which almost everything is suggested and almost nothing happens. I quote this judgment sometimes as if it were my own discovery. Whether accurate or not, it has the ring of profundity. Mostly I think it's a lot of shit what people say about books, just words to fill the empty spaces. I'm pretty good at shooting a certain kind of literary shit myself before a friendly audience, though with teachers and fathers I can barely put together a complete sentence. I signal to a stewardess as she goes up the aisle, holding up the Coors can to indicate I'd like another. "Someone will be taking your lunch order in a few minutes," she says, moving away, called invisibly to some other business. I read somewhere (or am I making that up too?) that stewardesses have sex all the time on the ground because it reminds them of being in the air.

I don't recall my father talking to me about his own work, though he had opinions about almost everything else. I don't know why it was so, but we tended to avoid the subject of books altogether. Sometimes as a joke I would say to him, "Write any good books lately?" I don't remember what he answered; he may not have said anything at all. Our main topics of conversation were movies and sports (baseball and basketball mostly) and how I was doing in school. He was full of theories about winning and losing that always seemed to me beside the point. "If they weren't committed to losing," he'd say about some team we supported, "they'd find some way to win." "Doesn't everyone want to win?" I'd ask. "It's dangerous to get what you want," my father would say. "You don't understand that , do you?" I'd nod as though I understood, but then a little later the question would come out, "What happens to you if you get what you want?" Then he would explain or he wouldn't, and it would make no difference which, his explanation beyond my reach, that it was death-bent to challenge the gods. (Could the gods field an entire team? I used to wonder). The teams that didn't want to win—they were always somehow ours—lacked character, he would say. The teams my father supported were underdogs of degraded character, frightened to the point of ineptitude at the distant prospect of victory. I didn't always enjoy going to games with him. When his team was losing he could be embarassing to be around, complaining about the referees in a self-pitying voice that made me want to pretend I didn't know him. "It's just a game," I would say, giving him back his own wisdom of an earlier day. "They're calling them all against us," he'd say. "They won't give us a break." He would calm down for moments but the slightest turn against his interests would set him off again. It was like being with a madman. Then there were times he held me responsible for his teams' failures as if I had some magic I was refusing to employ on his behalf. I took it to heart, began to root secretly against his teams, wanted to see them fail because of his stake in their success. If I couldn't will them to victory, I could at least take pleasure in their defeat. My own theory: a man committed to losers got what he deserved.

It is not one time but several times coming together as one. Not memories but invention, as he would say, given the shape and condition of recollection. I know it is my father before I am fully awake. His heavy walk rings the floors. My mother asks him to leave in a soft reasonable voice, says she doesn't want the children's sleep disturbed. He says—I am pressed agaist the closed door of my room—that he has as much right to be in the house as she. He won't stay long, he says in a wheedling voice, he just wants to see his kids for a few minutes. Be a sport, Magda.

You don't want them to see you like this, she says.

Like what? I wonder and open the door to see for myself.

Is this your idea of seeing the kids? she asks. He has her backed against a wall, his arms out.

She slips out from under his arms. I think you should leave, she says. Goodbye.

He has his arms around her. Let's go into your room, he says, kissing her, my mother drawing back her head.

The children will wake up, she says. I want you to leave.

They are out of view when I hear her say in a loud whisper, I don't want to, don't you understand.

They go into her bedroom and close the door.

The man next to me is asleep, his mouth open, a faint sound coming from him, an industrial hum. I get up to go to the bathroom, slide by two sets of knees. The plane lurches slightly. A child lets out a heart-breaking cry. In the bathroom cubicle, after peeing, I stand slumped over the bowl, waiting out a bout of nausea. When it passes—it is as if it never quite arrives—I have the illusion that I glimpse my father's face in the mirror. Actually there's hardly a resemblance between us, except perhaps at the mouth, in the thin red line of the lips. On the face in the mirror, sweat sprouts like a rash. I am allergic to small enclosures, to other people's reflections staring back at me. I wash my face and hands, comb my hair, flush the toilet, the poisonous liquid raining thirty thousand feet into the ocean.

I have this idea off and on that my life is a movie or made up of pieces of old movies. A girl about my own age stops me as I step out of the bathroom, says amazing as it may sound her travelling companion, a lady named Mrs. Karp, had gone up front about twenty minutes ago to get a magazine and hasn't returned. She has searched the entire plane and there is no sign of her friend. I don't know what to believe, suspect the girl is on something, but her story as she tells it is full of convincing detail. When I get back to my seat I begin to wonder if there isn't, as she suspects, some kind of conspiracy aboard this plane. She sits, empty seat next to her, with her hands over her face.

It often strikes me that almost everything we take for granted is something of a fraud. I'm not dogmatic about my conclusions. One thing is true for me at one moment and another, maybe the opposite, is true the next. We are suspended in the air, going nowhere; the plane is going on course at the speed represented by the pilot. The girl in the Grateful Dead sweatshirt has lost her friend on the plane; there is no friend and never was. My father wants to see me and my father wants to get rid of me. I am making this trip to see my father; I am making this trip to see what my father wants.

Once the connections break, it is hard to put things together again.

I feel at times like an old man, older than my father, as if I had already lived through my future on some secret wave length. My mother likes to say that her friends think of me as an adult, forget when talking to me that I'm her little boy. Someone had to take his place, I suppose, and after the first few years there was no one else. It's like it's so far back I can't remember having been a child. I mean, I don't know if I even had a childhood. I just turned eighteen and I haven't the faintest idea what it was like to be twelve.

My mother won't say anything directly, but I know she feels he's ruined her life. I've never gotten anything from him either, not anything I've ever wanted. For some reason this complaint always fits itself into the same words as if it existed independent of any specific reality. When I think of him I say to myself: *I've never gotten anything from my father.* It's always the same words, the feeling stuck in the same flag of language. I've never got anything real from him. All the time I've spent with him has been wasted time. I don't expect anything from him; I don't really want anything from him. All of this, which I know to be true, rings false. Language, which is his weapon, has put me in a false position. Who's to blame for that? Sometimes I think I could kill him for putting me in the wrong.

My father wears on this occasion a three piece tobacco-brown corduroy suit with the texture of velvet. He is two years late for our appointment. We go to a restaurant called Toros, which is a hangout for writers and literary groupies. My father is fussed over by the proprietor, a hard-bitten type who professes to admire everyone's work, and we are conducted to our table like visiting dignitaries.

"How's school?" my father asks.

"It's okay," I say. "As a matter of fact I've stopped going."

He nods, refuses to comment, purses his lips in disapproval.

"Do you know who that is?" he asks, pointing to a red-faced man in a belted leather jacket at a table perhaps ten feet from ours. The man, being pointed at, looks up, nods to my father, says something amusing to his companion.

"Do you see that man?" my father asks, his harsh whisper too loud not to be overheard. He mentions a name vaguely known to the general public, a figure of minor celebrity. "He was functionally illiterate until he was twenty-five. The man couldn't write a business letter, could barely spell his own name. He was working in the garment district in New York as an assistant buyer and he had a nervous breakdown. He began writing as a form of therapy. His wife, Minerva, who was a high school English teacher, edited his manuscript into recognizable English, taught him the rules of English syntax."

"Dad, he can hear you," I say, speaking behind my hand.

"Doesn't matter. He knows what I'm saying is true. After he made a lot of money—on his third book if I remember—he left Minerva and the kids for a seventeen year old girl. The girl was at most a year older than his oldest daughter whose name unless I'm mistaken was Loretta. The man hasn't written a creditable book since then because he has no one to rewrite them for him. Critics take the cramp in his syntax for evidence of a deepening of purpose. The truth is, he's unable to write a lucid sentence."

The object of my father's cruel description is talking in an equally loud whisper about my father. I hear the name Lukas Terman rise and fall in the buzz of the room.

A couple come to the table to greet my father. "I want you to meet my son, Tom," he says.

"Your father's the best writer in this room," the man says.

"Is that right?"

"He's also the sexiest man in the room," the woman says, kissing my father on the cheek.

"That's the nicest compliment of all," he says.

When the couple move off to their own table, I ask my father if they are writers too.

"In a manner of speaking," he says in his loud whisper. "Talented beginners. The girl has a telling way with a phrase but doesn't know when enough is enough. The man can speak in tongues but hasn't yet found his own voice.... Tell me why you aren't going to school."

"I don't know why," I say.

The answer seems to close the subject for the moment. His attention moves elsewhere. He gives me a brief biography of a bearded man standing with his back to us at the bar.

"Do you know everyone in the room?" I ask.

The waiter comes over and my father asks him what's good. "Everything," the waiter says, winking at me.

"As I don't have to tell you, everything also means nothing." says my father. "Isn't that so?"

"In this restaurant, everything means everything. What do you want me to tell you? You want me to tell you bluefish, I'll tell you bluefish."

"Is it fresh?"

"Like my daughter's tongue," he says.

They joke back and forth like characters in a play or a movie made out of a play. I have the idea that there are cameras filming them, that hidden microphones record their conversation.

When the waiter finally goes off with our order, my father asks me what I think of him.

"He's not very fast," I say. "He talks too much."

"What I'm asking is if you recognize him," my father says. "He looks familiar, doesn't he?"

"Yeah. Well, I don't know. Where would I have seen him?"

"He's a comedian. He used to do commercials on television."

I'm willing to believe his other stories—it's like not bothering not to believe them—but not this one. "I've never seen him on television," I say.

"He used to be on all the time," says my father. "You couldn't turn on the set without catching him doing something. He was a man of a thousand faces and two thousand voices. He was a brilliant comic, too brilliant for his own good. Viewers tended to remember his persona and not the product he was selling. The agency that was using him let him go—there was some scandal in the background as well. When they tried to hire him back he refused their offer. He would not be bought off by any amount of money. Besides, he liked being a waiter at Toros, liked the idea of having a secret, of being other than he seemed."

"Well," I say, skeptical to the last,"maybe when he was working as a comedian he was realy a waiter in disguise."

No one is what he seems. Everyone in the restaurant, guest or employee, has an astonishing private history, which my father reveals to me in his blaring whisper.

Lunch is being served. Though I think of passing it up this trip, the stewardess vetoes my decision by letting down my little table and serving me.

For the last year or so I've been incredibly impassive, sitting still for whatever comes by, unable to put one foot in front of another without being told I had no other choice. Lunch sits in front of me on a plastic tray and I pick at it—not the swiss steak but the potato puff and the salad—trying to determine whether I'm really hungry or only filling time. The man next to me lights up a cigarette to accompany his second cup of coffee. A woman of about my mother's age turns around to tell him that there is no smoking allowed in this section. My neighbor takes two more drags before snuffing out the cigarette.

"Thank you," the woman says with heavy sarcasm. "It only took you four hours to get the message."

"What message is that, lady?" he asks, winking at me. "If my smoking bothered you, why didn't you say something before?"

The woman, who is English, offers him the back of her head, says nothing that we can hear. An unintelligible whine of complaint hangs in the air. She turns once again and says, "The rules are made for some, I dare say, and not for others."

"What is she talking about?" he says to me. "We've been in the air close to five hours and I've smoked two cigarettes, really half of two cigarettes. Does that make me a public nuisance?"

He can't let go. Even after he opens his attaché case to get at some business documents he's already read three or four times he continues to justify himself. I turn my face to the window, make no response. "Am I being unreasonable?" he asks me.

"Everything's unreasonable," I say.

Do I surprise him? He accepts the remark not as intended, but as a gesture of empathy, the men against the woman, the Americans against the English. "You most of all," I could have added, though stopped short of saying what I meant.

When the trays are cleared away, the panel in front of our section lifts up to reveal a screen. We are requested to draw the shades over the windows and to put out the pintpoints of light overhead. I seem to be the only one in my immediate area without headphones, had probably been sleeping when the stewardess offered them for sale.

I watch the movie without sound a while, which has its own interest. It concerns a retired rodeo star who is reduced to making drunken public appearances on behalf of an unlikely breakfast cereal. After a scene with in which the cowboy, too drunk to go throuh his paces, watches an impersonator perform in his place, I close my eyes, let them close. The movie washes over me.

The multi-national company that manufactures the cereal with the cowboy's pictures on the box also has in its employ an international ring of assassins. One of them has been assigned "to terminate" the cowboy's career. The assassin, however, makes the crucial mistake of perceiving the false cowboy as the real one. I wake before the scenario can play itself out, the assassin waiting in ambush for the false cowboy's scheduled arrival.

What will the real cowboy do when he learns that his double has been killed in his place?

In the real movie the cowboy redeems his debased life by trekking through beautiful countryside accompanied by a woman and a horse, avoiding unseen pursuers.

The plane begins its descent, stuttering slightly as it falls, the sky darker as we come closer to the earth. I reach in my jacket pocket for a stick of gum, come out empty-handed. Ears ache as if wooden nails had been driven into the drums on each side. I am not ready to come down.

I can imagine my father, beardless with two days growth, sitting in one of these black director's chairs, his legs crossed, an unattended cigarette smoking in the ashtray. He is going through the manuscript of a screenplay, making notes to himself in the margin with a red pen.

The ending isn't right, isn't right as an ending or isn't right as the last scene of this particular film. It's even possible that the ending is not at fault in itself but symptomatic of the failure of the whole work. My father has been too long on this screenplay to know, has lost all sense of balance. His watch, which he glances at to gauge the time he has before leaving for the airport, has stopped, something he won't discover until hours later. If he intends to take the car to Heathrow, he'll have to leave the house in fifteen minutes, he thinks, though in fact he is already several minutes late.

The plane comes out of its descent, begins to level off, offers the illusion of rising again. The man next to me says that he heard there was an Air Traffic Controller's strike at Heathrow and that we would have difficulty landing.

"What a bore!" one of the English ladies in front of us says.

I am in no hurry, consider the possibility of the plane hanging around for awhile. It's been my limited experience that anything is possible. The fantasy wills itself. One of the emergency doors is suddenly blown open and everything not nailed down is sucked into the maelstrom of the sky, three hundred or so passengers dropping into London like a rain of hailstones.

I try to imagine what it would be like to fall into my father's life like a bomb.

2

In the final scene, his hero, the international detective Henry Berger, would track the conspiracy to some unnamed European country and into a palace of mirrors to be cut down at gun point as he enters the building by the one person he continues to trust. The film would stop just as the bullet struck him, or fractionally before, a look of astonishment and disillusion on Henry Berger's face, the reflection of it echoing through the maze of the room. "I love it," Max Kirstner said, "but is it, I wonder, absolutely on the mark? Irony tempered by human understanding. This script must be beyond bloody reproach, my friend, or so subversive that the sharpest accountant in the industry doesn't know he's being had. What it wants at this stage is a touch more compassion." He spoke, particularly when the news was bad, at astonishing speed.

Terman agreed to study the director's notes and the inane jottings of some producer's reader, which is to say he kept his disagreement unspoken. A year ago almost to the day, Max had pronounced the screenplay "beautiful beyond my wildest hopes." "A few cosmetic changes," the director had said, "and we're in business, son." Three drafts later—it was a collaboration in which Terman did the writing and the director suggested other possibilities—they seemed only infinitesimally closer to a shooting script. With each revision, new problems of strucure and conception arose. Someone who mattered—sometimes it was Terman himself—was always unsatisified.

He was revising the closure, had put Henry Berger, and the unnamed woman with whom he traveled, on a flight from London to New York. He was due at Heathrow himself in little over an hour. Before leaving for the airport, he called Isabelle at the most recent work number she had given him, wanting to heal the wounds of the previous night. She wasn't at that number, he was told, after having been held on the line for ten minutes, was working today at some other studio. Did they have another number for her? They didn't or were opposed to giving it out, kept him waiting as they debated the issue outside his hearing. If they wouldn't give out her number, would they call her themselves and say that Lukas Terman was trying to reach her? The woman on the other end said that it was not a question of not wanting to give out a number but of not having a number to give out. He didn't believe it, said, overstating, that it was an urgent matter, that the news he had for Isabelle was something she had been waiting to hear. "That's not my problem, is it?" said the woman. "I'll take down your number. That's the best I can do."

He wrote Isabelle a note in case she returned in his absence and propped it up with a paperweight against the phone in the kitchen.

Deciding she might go right by it if she were in a hurry, he took it up to their bedroon and laid it out on her pillow, though he was not fully satisfied with that placement either. After going down the stairs, after putting on his corduroy jacket, he returned to the bedroom to retrieve the note, reading it as if with Isabelle's eyes.

> Dear I,
> Gone to Heathrow to get Tom. Sorry about last night. Put it down to gracelessness under pressure, or try to imagine it never happened. I regret my behavior and admire your forebearance. I mean to do better in the future. Love—
>
> Terman

He was out the door with the note folded in his jacket pocket when he thought to go back and leave it on the kitchen table. The details of his return were exactly as he had imagined them: the undoing of the bolt lock, retracting the catch with second key, going through the front parlor (that enormous room), into back parlor, into dining room, taking a right turn into the kitchen, putting the note down on the table where it couldn't be missed, a butter knife across it to hold it in place, then the same trip in reverse order, remembering to double lock from the outside, hurrying to his car.

Driving to the airport through unyielding traffic, he decided that the note was an ill-conceived gesture, that Isabelle would more readily forgive him if he hadn't apologized than if he had. It was also possible that, taking him at his word, she wouldn't return to the house at all. He had suggested (the suggestion seeming to make itself), that she spend the first night or two of Tom's visit at her own place.

"It makes a lot of sense,"she said and went up to the bedroom to pack a few things.

He found her sitting on the bed in an uncharacteristically crumpled posture, an empty suitcase on her lap. "It'll only be for a day or two," he said.

"Thank you," she said in a hurry.

"What are you thanking me for?" She tended to express gratitude at the most inappropriate moments, a source of small irritation to him.

"For being straightforward with me." Her lip quivered. She was not given to excesses.

He took the suitcase from her lap and sat with her in silence, his arm draped around her shoulders, until it was time to go to bed.

"If you don't mind, I want to stay at my own place tonight," she said. "You won't make it difficult for me, will you?"

"Does it make it difficult if I say I don't want you to go?"

"Of course it does," she said. "You damn well asked me to leave, didn't you?"

He repeated her name in exasperation, a litany of Isabelles.

The signs pointing him to the airport led him there. As he entered the building, his doomsday premonitions slipped away. The first thing he did was to go to the bathroom to empty his bladder of, as it turned out, illusion. His hair was in terminal disarray, and he wet it down, combing it with his hand, which was no improvement. He had a rash on his forehead, a portent of bad weather from within. When he got out of the bathroom he followed the signs to Immigration and lined up on the other side of the rope to wait for Tom. There were four booths out of a possible nine in operation, passengers from a mix of two or three flights filtering through. Terman hated to wait, hated to stand in one place without other occupation, suffered loss of time as if it were (as it is) an incurable disease. He memorized the faces of people coming through, committed to not missing a thing, dimly worried that he might not recognize his son. Who can explain associations? It struck him that the grail (was that his idea of Tom?) only revealed itself to the pure in heart. He interrupted his vigil from time to time to check his watch which, it suddenly dawned on him, had had the same time for the past two hours. He could almost admire its constancy.

"I know you," a woman said to him. She had come up to him from the blind side, surprising him in an unacceptable way. "You may not remember me."

"No," he said, not looking at her. "I don't."

"Aren't you Lukas Terman? You knew me as Lila Parsicki. My

former husband and I lived in the same building as you and your wife—I mean of course your former wife. A lot of water has passed under the bridge since then."

He looked at her for the briefest of moments, withheld recognition. "You have the wrong bridge," he said, affecting a faint European accent.

"I'm sorry to have interfered with your privacy," she said in a sarcastic voice, offering him a view of her back. Though physically round, heavy-breasted, moon-faced, big-hipped, her manner was all angles and sharp points. He remembered her with marked displeasure, and moved away into the underbrush of the crowd.

The moment he forgot about her, she was at his elbow again. "You shouldn't lie to people," she said. "It's not the least bit nice."

"Excuse me," he said in his mock-German accent.

She thrust her face into his, as close as it might get given that he was six or seven inches taller. "I said I don't like to be lied to," she said.

He regretted his imposture, though he was unwilling to give it up, stared ahead blindly, neglecting his relentless vigil.

There was no sign of Tom as far as he could see and Terman reasoned the boy had missed the plane, or had decided at the last possible moment not to make the trip. His reaction to the possibility of Tom's not coming at all—relief perhaps one aspect of it—was without definition. Terman also wondered whether it was conceivable that Tom had passed through without being recognized by his father.

Lila joined the people she was with, then—her tenacity frightening and marvelous—returned to his ear. "Is it that you're hiding from someone?" she asked. "Believe me, I have no intention of revealing your innermost secrets."

The more he ignored her, the more lethal her voice became. "Don't you think it's cruel to pretend not to know someone? It's the most awful thing, believe me, to have your view of reality denied. Are you trying to make me doubt my whole system of perception? Is that your intention? I can't believe you'd be so heartless."

Even if she were in the right—surely the crowd must recognize that—her reaction was far in excess of provocation. He strove for a posture of heroic (and compassionate) indifference.

"It's not true that he doesn't know me," she said in a strident voice, attracting the embarrassed attention of a half a dozen people around them. "It's not true and he knows it's not true."

She went on in the same vein, pleading her case to a circumstantial jury, increasing the stakes of her complaint. He had ruined a number of women, she said, had humiliated them in unimaginable ways. Terman stared at the floor, refused to acknowledge that the outburst of this impossible woman concerned him.

As gratuitously as she started her assault, Lila gave it up. The potentiality of its return filled the air like some unaccountable hum. When he felt he could do it inconspicuously, he looked around to see where she had gone. Their eyes met—she had been waiting for him to seek her out—and she mouthed, "I'm still here."

He had a momentary loss of focus where he had to remind himself why he was there, studying the illegible faces of people he didn't know and was not likely to see again. The crowd thinned and after awhile he discovered himself its sole survivor. Even Lila had gone on to other business. It seemed uncanny that he and Tom should miss connection.

He had Thomas Terman paged over the loudspeaker and when he heard the mostly familiar name in the air, he had the urge to answer the call himself.

The international long distance lines were oversubscribed and Terman had to wait for the longest time before he could get his call through to New York.

"Is something wrong?"Magda asked as soon as she recognized the voice.

"I was going to ask you the same question. Did Tom make his flight?"

She sighed, a woman who valued competence above all other virtues. "As far as I know. Isn't he there with you?"

"You saw him board the plane?"

"I would have heard from him by now if he hadn't gotten on. How could you have missed him?"

"Magda, he wasn't there. I waited for him at Immigration for over an hour."

She made a groaning sound. "You'd better do something to find him. If you want my advice, that's what it is."

His pose of sensible concern at great distance from what he really felt, he said, "I'll keep in touch, Magda."He swallowed the name.

She said nothing he could hear, withdrawing from the connection like someone backing out a door.

He had Tom paged one more time. The call produced Lila Parsicki who sidled up to him just as he was leaving the Pan Am desk. She thought he ought to know, she said, moments before he arrived someone who resembled the Tom she remembered, though he was just a child when she'd seen him last, had passed through Immigration and gone on without stopping. "What did he look like?" Terman asked.

"He had the same blue eyes as Magda," she said.

It was not impossible. Terman reconstructed the scene. Not seeing his father as he came through Immigration and unsure of the arrangements they had made, Tom had assumed that he was supposed to go on to his father's house in London and had proceeded accordingly. The misunderstanding was grave but forgivable. With barely a nod of thanks to Lila for her information, he hurried off to his car and fought his way back through traffic in half the time of the original trip.

The Holland Park house was dark on his return and Terman rang the bell to no answer before letting himself in with his key. He made himself a double Scotch with Perrier water, sat down on the least comfortable chair in the front parlor and wondered what steps a man in his situation ought to take next.

A few minutes after he decided that the next move was Tom's the phone rang. It took him a while to answer, undecided as to which extension to pursue, though he was naturally eager to get the news.

The voice was not the one he expected so diasappointed him, the disappointment mingled with relief. It was Isabelle's husky purr at his ear. She was staying with a friend in Battersea, would see him, she said, tomorrow or the day after. He didn't urge her return, although it was a recurrent intention. "I can't live without you," he said to her at some point, which produced a moan or a laugh. No mention was made of his son,no questions asked.

He sat up by the phone in his study, kept close watch on it, awaiting Tom's call, but after a while he dozed in his chair and when he woke up it was the next day.

#

The morning passed without word from Tom. The only call had been from Max Kirstner to remind him of an appointment at his office for two that afternoon. Terman didn't mention Tom's disappearance, said he would be by as arranged, though when he was off the horn he had the distinct recollection that their appointment had been for the following day. Max never had to change his mind; he just revised the past.

The fourth complete version of the "The Folkestone Conspiracies" was opened in front of him on the desk and though he couldn't bear to look at the screenplay again, he read through the opening scene.

THE FOLKSTONE CONSPIRACIES
Screenplay by Max Kirstner and Lukas Terman

The screen is gray, almost black. If we look closely enough, we can make out the silhouette of a man. He could be anyone. He seems to be speaking, though perhaps the voice comes from elsewhere.

Voice: I cannot reveal my identity to you at this time. If it were known that I was telling you this story, I would be permanently silenced, rubbed out as if I were no more substantial than a typographical error. I mention this so that you will excuse the rudeness of my not showing my face. The story I am to tell is true, as true as any story you're likely to be told in the dark. My connection to these events is not important. Let it be said that I had a seat on the periphery of the action. The story starts—I was about to say our story, but unfortunately the story at the moment is mine alone—in a European country known for its neutrality in international affairs. A shabby, unprepossing man of early middle age, rumored to have some connection with Interpol, has arrived this morning and taken a room in the capital city's second finest hotel. On his visa where it says profession, he has written "Journalist." Where it say purpose of visit, he has written "Holiday."

The gray screen seems to be a curtain and is pulled open to reveal the registration desk of the Hotel Candide.

Attendant: You are in Room 917, Monsieur Berger. The room you request is occupé, though you will find the one we have given you has nothing to be said against it.

Berger: Who may I ask is Room 1017?

Attendant: It is in the process of renovation.

We cut abruptly to the small elevator as Henry Berger gets in. As the doors close, we see a tall man wearing dark purple gloves, his face obscured, say something to the desk clerk. The clerk looks puzzled, shakes his head.

We see Henry Berger entering his hotel room. He tips the bellhop more than he expects, says: "My wife will be joining me later." When the bellhop leaves, Henry Berger walks to the window to check the view. He puts his suitcases on the bed, opens one of them, takes out a change of shirt and then, as if an afterthought, a small revolver which he rests next to the shirt. He walks around the large room, looking for something—a bugging device, it soon becomes apparent—and seems disappointed not to find one. He then picks up the phone and makes a call.

Woman's voice: Si?

Henry Berger: Let me speak to Carlos Soto, please.
Woman: Not here.
Berger: Is there some place I could reach him? I'm an old friend.
Woman: He has no old friends. There is no place to reach him.
Berger: I wouldn't be calling unless it were important.
Woman: Leave your name and place and he will locate you.

Henry Berger gets into a taxi, gives the driver an address, and settles back into his seat. After a moment, he has an intuition and glances out the back window to see a black limousine keeping pace. They turn a corner and the limousine, some fifteen yards behind, also turns. Henry Berger insructs the cab driver to do what he can to shake the car behind them. The driver, after initial confusion, says: "You mean the way do in Amercian movies? I do my best for you." The cab makes an abrupt left turn at the next corner, then speeds two blocks and turns left again. In a few seconds the limousine reappears in pursuit. The driver says that he has not shown them his best yet. After narrowly avoiding a collision with a truck—this after a succession of hairpin turns—the cab loses its pursuer. Berger looks at his watch, shakes his head despairingly at the loss of time.

Cut to Berger going though the front doors of an apartment building that might have seemed elegant in the 1920's. There is an odd quiet in the building, the lobby (which has a fountain at the center) desolate. Berger takes the lift up, rings the buzzer at 50, waits, rings again, tries the door. The door is open and he goes in, calling "Carlos?... Carlos?" There is no answer, no sound of life. The stub end of a cigarette, however, is still burning in an ash tray. The bedroom door is closed and Berger knocks on it twice before going in. He stops after taking two steps into the room, turns his head. We see at a blurred distance, as if Berger were glancing at them out of the corner of his eye, the corpses of a man and a woman on the bed. Berger is profoundly upset, sits down in the living room at the edge of the sofa. A matchbook on a coffee table catches his eye—Cafe Fleurs de Mal, he reads upside down....

#

A knock at the front door—perhaps it was the fifth or sixth knock—recalled his attention.

He let himself out of the study—the door sticking briefly—and hurried down the long flight of stairs, wondering why his visitor had overlooked the bell. It was the kind of knock that policemen in movies made in the middle of the night.

He thought he knew who it was even before he opened the door to let his son in.

Tom stood there, frowning apologeticaly, his swollen canvas suitcase a foot or so behind as if it had trailed him there without his notice. He had the look of someone who didn't plan to stay.

Terman waited a moment before inviting him in, frozen himself in the doorway, considered embracing his son, cosidered taking his hand, considered acknowledging some pleasure in his presence, but found himself committed to silence and inaction. He remembered an appointment he had and asked Tom if he knew the time.

"Am I too late?" Tom asked.

Terman went behind his son to gather up the lone suitcase—was that all there was?—and asked in passing where he had been, mumbled the question.

"Let me take that," Tom said, pulling it from his father, the case suspended momentarily between them, the object of a tug of war. Terman gave it up and Tom carried the suitcase in himself.

"I don't know how I missed you," Terman said. "If it was my fault, I apologize."

Tom dropped heavily into a chair, the springs crunching under his sudden weight. "It's not too comfortable," he said. "It's not the lap of luxury so to speak."

Terman took the rebuke personally, indicated that the larger of the two couches was the most reasonable place to sit, a piece of information Tom acknowledged with a nod, though he didn't trouble himself to move. Perhaps he liked being uncomfortable, Terman thought, perhaps that's what he wanted. "Did you spend the night in a hotel?" he asked him.

"No," Tom said.

"Where were you all night?"

Tom studied the question from all sides. "Around," he said.

Where did the time go? Terman noticed that it was already after two (seven minutes after) and he phoned Max to say he had been detained unavoidably. "Tell you the truth, I've forgotten why I wanted to see you," Max said. "No doubt it will all come back to me in a blinding light when you get here. How's young Oedipus making out?" When Terman got off the phone, Tom had his eyes closed.

He was going to shake him but discovered he was reluctant to put his hand on the boy's shoulder. "Tom" he whispered. "Tom."

"Sleepy," the boy murmured, the voice dredged from some pocket of childhood.

"Tom," he whispered, "your room is on the third floor, second door to the left from the main stairway. I have to go out a while on business. There's some cheese in the refrigerator, stilton and brie, which should tide you over if you get hungry. Will you be all right?"

There was no response from the sleeping form, barely the sound of breathing. The boy had a mustache or the beginnings of one, yet seemed younger than his age, seemed with his eyes pressed shut like a fearful and vulnerable child. Terman took a blanket from the hall closet, a faded pink blanket that might have come with the house or been donated by Isabelle for some occasion he disremembered, and put it over Tom's lap.

"Tom," he said, standing over the sleeping figure, unwilling or unable to leave, "I'm going now."

It was twenty-five to three and he took a taxi, despite feelings of impoverishment, so as not to be any later than was already unavoidable. The days went too quickly, he thought, moved in accelerated time, didn't know when to stop. He was forty only last year and in less than a month he would be forty-five. Where had his life gone?

Max's secretary, Valerie Lowe, reputed also to be his mistress, had her hand on his shoulder, was shaking him with unreasonable zeal. He had been getting layed in a cathouse in some obscure town in Idaho while waiting for his car to be gassed. When rude hands were laid on him."You were snoring obscenely," Valerie said.

Two men of a certain age were coming out of Max Kirstner's office, expensive suits, one of whom, an investor in films, Terman had met before.

The other, a hawk-faced man, prematurely white-haired, came over and shook hands. "Luke Terman, is it? I'm a great fan of yours."

Terman aspired to conceal his dislike for his ostensible admirer, took the other's hand. "What a coincidence," he said. "I happen also to be a fan of yours."

"Mutual admiration society, are we? I doubt you even know my name."

"I may not know your name," he said, "but I have your number."

When the men were gone Max apologized in his perfunctory way for having kept Terman waiting in the anteroom. "I'm not my own man," he said. This remark, which he used at every opportunity, self-parodying and ingratiating as it seemed, was an excuse, Terman knew, that permitted Max almost anything.

"Whose man are you this week?" Terman asked.

Max looked over his shoulder in parody of a man pursued. "Let's repair to the inner sanctum," he said out of the side of his mouth.

Terman trailed his employer and collaborator into the elegantly cluttered inner office, sat down before invited to.

Max took out a bottle of brandy and two coffee mugs from his desk—it was the way they always started—and poured them both a drink. "Do you have anything for me?"

"I thought it was you who had something for me."

Max laughed with his mouth closed, took a thick nine by twelve envelope from his desk and placed it in Terman's hands. "Take a look."

"Must I?"

"You bloody well must," he said, making an ironic face at the ceiling. "You'll love it, old son. It's from the fine Italian hand of the producer's nephew."

He knew his line. "I've seen the fingerprints before," he said.

"They want us to go into production in ten days," Max said casually, watching him out of the side of his eye. "We can't do that, can we?"

"I thought all the money wasn't in place."

Max put his feet up on the desk. "For the sake of argument, let us say the money is there, a proposition we both know to be contrary to fact. If it were all there, could we or could we not begin principal shooting in ten days? Is the screenplay, in your opinion, ready to be shot?"

"Whenever you're ready to shoot it, it's ready to be shot," Terman said, his irritation undisguised. "You're the director." He had the sense that they had had this same conversation, almost to a word, six months ago.

"Terman, Terman," Max said, spoke his name as if he were a recalcitrant child that needed shaking, shook him by his name, loosed his name in the air between them, pointed a finger at him. "If it weren't your script, Terman, what would you advise? I put myself in your hands."

Terman looked at his hands. "They're empty," he said.

Max pantomimed exasperation, poured them both another brandy. "What are we talking about? Is it your perception of reality, old son, that I don't want this film to happen? Can you honestly accuse me of faint-heartedness on this project? Have I not been Henry Berger's most enthusiastic supporter but one from the outset? I issue no blame but the script, which I think is basically terrific, has never been quite on target, has it?"

Terman stood up to say that he disliked being manipulated, was prepared to walk out, though he sat down again with only the barest murmur of complaint. He had the sense that Max understood him, that what wasn't said was in its own way made known.

The subject changed, or evolved into something else without

appearing to change. "I want this film to transcend its apparent occasion," Max was saying. "This isn't a genre film we're making, is it? We're dealing here, as you know, with a transcendent conspiracy, a cosmic malevolence. Okay? If all the agencies of civilization are corrupt and murderous, we have to offer the viewer some kind of moral counterweight. That's the missing element. Do you see my point?"

Terman had a sense of déjâ vu comparable to walking into a movie you had dreamed or seen before under another title, though Max often generated that illusion in him. The director made a self-deprecating gesture then laughed at himself.

"Marjorie's been longing to have you and Isabelle over for a feast," Max said. That unfulfilled expectation had been in the air between them for months.

"We've been waiting to be asked over," Terman said. "We talk of nothing else."

"I'm going to hold you to that," Max said. "Some people are coming to the house in Kent for the long weekend and I want you and Isabelle to join the party. It would give you and me the opportunity to make finishing touches on the script mano a mano."

"Not this weekend, Max," Terman said. "My son just arrived and I really have to spend some time with him."

"No problem there," said Max. "Thing to do is bring the prodigal along." The director got up, a whimsical finger in the air—some further comment held in abeyance—and went into the bathroom adjoining the office.

Had he been dismissed? Terman got up to go, though not before overhearing the splashes of Max's disemburdening in some secret place behind the wall.

"You'll have to give me directions," he said to the closed door.

"You just follow your nose," said Max.

Driving back to the Holland Park house, he wondered what Tom was up to in his absence and conceived a scenario.

#

Even after Tom heard the door close, even after he imagined his father getting into his car and driving off, even then he kept his eyes closed for another ten or fifteen minutes, focusing on a swatch of light that seemed to burn through the blackness. He conceived himself getting out of his chair, his eyes still tightly shut, like a spirit stepping out of its body. His spirit didn't go far without him, it never had.

The house was even bigger than he had imagined and more bizarre, one inexplicable place moving anomalously into another. He knew from his father's letters that certain movies had been filmed there, but the odd thing was how different the mood of each of the rooms, how startlingly unrelated to one another. He decided to see it all, to take the full tour, starting on the third floor and working his way down. The room set aside for him was at the far end of the hall—it was the third room he had visited, the only one with a freshly made bed—and looked, he thought, like someone's idea of a 19th century French whorehouse. The bed was too soft. There were pink cupids on the oval ceiling. The plush carpet was a garish red and with the overhead light on gave the impression of something recently eviscerated. On one of the two desks was a Blue Guide to London, a Nicholson's London Street Guide, and a map of the underground system. On the other was a set of two keys. He wondered why his father had chosen this particular room for him. Two of the rooms on the floor were more spacious, another had a more interesting view, still another was more appropriately furnished. Of the five unused bedrooms on the third floor, his was, taking a variety of factors into consideration, the third best overall. Who was the best room for, the room with mirrors on the walls and ceiling, an enormous space with a large round bed in the center and a terrace coming off one of the windows? He studied his reflection, reflection within reflection, in the several mirrors (odd, he thought, how unlike myself I am) then moved down to the second floor.

There were five rooms, not including bathrooms, on the second floor: his father's study, two bedrooms, an empty space, and a storage room with a padlock on the door. In this order, moving from left to right: study, storage room, bedroom, empty room, master bedroom. The first thing that struck him about the study was both wastebaskets were over-filled, a handful of scrunched up papers on the floor. He left the room, then tempted by something else, came back and sat down at his father's desk, swivelling absent-mindedly in the imitation leather chair. There was a blank sheet of paper in the typewriter. He typed "Every Good Boy Does Fine." Facing away from the desk, he reached behind him to open a drawer, the middle of three, his hand sidling in while his glance rested elsewhere. He came away with a black fountain pen the thickness of a fat cigar which he scrupulously returned. When he exhausted the middle drawer—there were no discoveries there, nothing but the obvious—he moved on to the drawer below. He worked his way through layers of manuscript to the bottom where he found the very thing he imagined himself looking for. And even then, moving it about with his fingers, grasping it, removing it from its secret place, he disbelieved his intuituion. He had only to turn his head slightly to verify the weapon he held in his hand, to verify that it was something other than a toy, but for the moment he resisted the discovery he would allow himself in the following moment. Having demonstrated a certain self-control, he rewarded himself by looking at the object in his hand. It was new, he thought, perhaps unused. It smelled faintly of oil and had an almost imperceptibly oily aspect. Tom watched himself in the mirror on the far wall, aiming his father's gun at the opposing figure. The sounds of bullets crashing against glass were only in his head,though from time to time he made small firing sounds in his throat, a muffled simulation of the real thing. It was childish, he knew, and he observed himself ironically pointing a pistol at the ironic observer that confronted him. The question of what the gun was for never asked itself and he was returning it to its place, trying to put it away exactly as it was found, when he was startled by the ringing of a doorbell. He put the gun and a box of shells in his jacket pocket and started down the stairs.

The doorbell rang a second and third time. Tom retraced his steps to the top of the stairs and waited anxiously for the intruder to decide that no one was home. The door opened—he could hear the turn of a key—and a woman came in. He couldn't quite see her face from his vantage at the top of the winding stairs but he had no doubts it was a woman. "Hallo," she called. "Is anyone there?"

"My father's not here,"he said, coming down.

A long-legged woman of about thirty or so appeared at the bottom of the wide stairwell. "Tom, is it?" she asked.

It was not something he was ready to deny. She introduced herself as Isabelle. "I'm Isabelle," she whispered. He thought of her—the words came to mind unbidden—as his father's whore, the latest and greatest. She looked like a movie star, he thought, somewhat like Julie Christie. "Do you live here with my father?" he asked.

She walked away, turned her back on him, before answering. "I have my own flat if it's any of your affair," she said.

"You came in with a key," he said.

He followed her into the kitchen and stood behind her at the stove while she waited for some water to boil, said he hadn't meant to be offensive.

"Of course you meant to be offensive,"she said.

"The hell with you," he said and sulked off.

She made herself a cup of tea which she drank in gulps while standing alongside the stove with her back to him.

"How do you know what my intention was?"he asked,his voice rising. Isn't it possible that you're the one who's being offensive?"

Isabelle was looking for something in a cabinet above the sink, her full concentration on whatever she sought.

After she left the kitchen, excusing herself to go by him, she went upstairs to the master bedroom. She was taking a hair dryer and some other gadgets from one of the dressers when Tom glanced in. "Does my father know you're doing that?" he asked.

She stopped what she was doing and stared cooly at him. "You're not to be believed, are you? You're just about the rudest person I've ever met in my life."

Tom walked out and came back, walked up the stairs and halfway down again. "Bitch," he whispered, a secret he was unwilling to share. She was the one not to be believed, he thought, a mean-spirited, presumptuous shrew. He was aware of having made a terrible impression.

He went upstairs to the unlikely room his father had given him and closed himself in with a self-dramatizing gesture. The door, that had appeared to bang shut, swung open. He crouched on the bed with his hand on the gun in his pocket, staring through tears into the shadows of the hall. His sense of grievance seemed a bottomless wound.

When he heard Isabelle leave he picked up one of the London guides, pocketed the set of keys (though he had no intention of returning) and, after taking a granny smith from the kitchen, let himself out. The house, particularly the third floor, spooked him.

He walked with his head down so was surprised to see Isabelle standing on the corner when he passed. She called to him or so he thought, hearing or imagining his name between them. "Tom?"

He didn't turn around, though considered the possibility.

"I didn't mean for us to get off so badly,"she said. "Sorry to be so shrill."

He turned and shrugged, felt himself immune to her seduction.

"Where are you off to?" she asked.

He withheld an answer, though it may only have been that he had none to give, shrugged his shoulders as if to say it's of no importance.

"You don't know or you're not telling?"

"Come on," he said. The kind of remark he would have made to his mother when he was fifteen. "I'm the rudest person you ever met in your life." He walked along with her, some small distance between them, into Holland Park.

It had never been his intention to accompany her; it was just that they happened to be going in the same direction, happened to be walking through an astonishing park across the street from his father's house.

They walked through a wooded path that screened out the sun, that seemed, for the few moments they were lost in its maze, like a dense forest. "Would you like to see the peacocks?" she asked him.

If he were capable of being charmed, the question would have charmed him.

He let her talk without offering anything in return, took pains to listen, was conscious of himself listening to her talk. At the same time—he rarely did fewer than two things at once—he found himself increasingly disturbed by the gun he had discovered in the bottom drawer of his father's desk. It was not something Terman would keep unless he had a use for it. What worried him most was his father's reaction when he discovered his revolver was missing.

She showed him the peacocks and he said yes, they were amazing. One of them had its feathers unfurled and was running up and back, making an odd threatening noise. She put a hand on his arm to gain his attention. She said she believed the noise was a mating call, that it stood to reason, didn't it? It seemed to him,he said, like some form of indigestion.

When they got to the other side of the park she said she had a flat nearby and did he want to stop in for a bite of something. The offer tempted him which was reason enough to turn it down. He said he planned to spend the day, what was left of it, checking out London.

"I know exactly what you mean," she said. "When I come to a new place I want to get some kind of hold on it. Is that how it is with you?"

"No," he said, then laughed madly.

He rejected her offer of food at least twice, stood in front of her building saying goodbye, before giving in to the afternoon's destiny. Isabelle put out a plate of jam tarts on the kitchen table and made a pot of tea. As an afterthought she brought out some stale bread and blue-veined cheese and the remains of a spinach salad decorated with slices of hard-boiled egg. Tom looked at the off-white walls of the small unlived-in apartment, said her taste reminded him somewhat of his mother's. There was one beer left in the otherwise bare refrigerator, a Watney's Light Ale, which Tom agreed to drink only if she would share it with him.

"Oh, Tom," she said, "go all the way."

He had a heel of bread, a tiny wedge of cheese and slightly more than a half a glass of ale and felt inescapably in her debt. Assuming that his father was what he wanted to talk about, she told him that

Terman, as everyone called him, was a difficult man to get to know, which he could have told her himself if she hadn't been the one telling it first.

"Does my father treat you badly?" he asked at one point.

She said no,at least not in the obvious way, that she was the difficult one or at least equally difficult.

He kept postponing his decision to leave until it seemed that if he didn't make his move momentarily, he might never get out the door.

"How did you meet him?" he asked.

"I don't know that I want to tell you that," she said.

He stood up abruptly, announced for the third or fourth time that he thought that he ought to go.

She said she understood, that she had to go somewhere in a few minutes herself.

Before he went out the door he thanked her for the food and they shook hands. She was as tall as he was (was it the heels she wore?) and their eyes met briefly in a way that frightened him.

Isabelle asked him, prolonging the awkward gesture of his departure, if he was pleased to be in London. He shrugged and said nothing, waving to her as he left, backing out the door, aware that he had expected something to happen between them that hadn't happened. He wondered what she made of his refusal to remove his coat.

He walked quickly, compelled to create some distance between himself and the occasion of his embarrassing performance. The neighborhood changed as he walked north, changed from street to street, a sense of obscure privilege slipping away, a failing of light.

Tom was looking in the window of a record shop when a young woman who resembled Isabelle, who at first he thought was Isabelle passed him in reflection. A moment later he saw her in a Newsagents shop—he was browsing in a magazine called *Time Out*—and listened in when the proprietor asked her about her father's condition.

She sighed before answering, her narrow figure weighted by trouble. "He came home from hospital yesterday," she said. "They say it will take a bit of time before he's himself."

"It's my opinion time heals all wounds," said the proprietor, an Indian or Pakistani. "Still, it's a terrible shame such things are allowed to happen."

When the girl left the shop Tom found himself walking in the same direction a few steps behind. He fell into the rhythm of her walk, mimicked her brisk, small steps. When she stopped to brush something from her skirt, he caught up with her despite an inclination to linger behind. He thought to introduce himself, felt pressured to talk, though passed her with only the barest stirring of words.

"Did you say something?" she asked.

Up close she was another person, someone less compelling than his first impression suggested. Her complexion was marred; her chin pointed oddly; her eyes were too close together. He resisted disappointment.

That she was less than beautiful made it easier for him to talk. He said what he had been rehearsing to say, that he had unwittingly overheard her remarks to the newsdealer and that he could understand how she felt about her father's illness, his own father having been a chronic invalid for years.

"How awful for you," she said.

"It's more mental than physical," Tom said. "He doesn't have memory of certain things—I mean obvious things like the names of people he's known all his life."

"That's a coincidence, isn't it?" she said without even the barest touch of irony. "My father's memory since his return from hospital is like a loose connection. He has flashes of clarity and then nothing. He has these dreams about the two thugs coming at him from behind and when he wakes up he's so frightened he doesn't know where he is. I have to sit with him until he gets back to sleep. He's like a little child."

Tom commiserated, said he knew exactly what she meant, that his own father was not without certain childish characteristics.

"You've lived with it longer than I have," she said. "Next to people who are really badly off, I account myself fortunate."

They walked a little further together, then she touched his shoulder and said she had to go in. "If I'm not there when he wakes up he goes into a panic," she said. He accompanied her to the door of the stunted frame house, noted that the address was 27 Foxglove Road. "What's your name?" he asked her.

She was suddenly distrustful. "Why do you want to know?"

"Yeah, well," he said. "A fatal attraction perhaps."

"That doesn't make much sense, does it?" she asked, her seriousness without flaw. "I'm not a pickup if that's what you're thinking."

"Forget it," he said.

She called something to him as he walked away, her name, which he didn't quite hear, which sounded like nothing he had ever heard before, the name of a flower perhaps. His face burned as if he had been slapped.

A church was being torn down at the next corner and he stopped for a moment to observe. The spire, supported by cables on three sides, was making its anxious descent, seemed possessed by some separate will. He noticed that one of the cables was frayed and trembling, looked as if it would snap at the smallest provocation. The workers seemed unconcerned with the potential danger. One in fact was smoking a cigarette with his back to the trembling cable. Tom called to him to look out. When he got no response—perhaps the danger was less than he imagined—he broke into a run, vaguely panicked by something. Two dark-skinned men were coming toward him in a way that seemed ominous. They opened a space for him to pass between them, a smallish space barely large enough to avoid contact. A slash of laughter pursued him. At some point he thought he heard the cable snap and an ancient voice cry out in pain or surprise. He never looked back.

He stopped at a fruit stand and bought a peach for ten pence. On the next street, a less disheartening one than the two preceding it, there was a Bed and Breakfast sign in one of the windows and, after passing the house, Tom returned to ring the bell.

A large distracted woman with chalky yellow hair led him to a small lightless room on the third floor, a single window offering a view of the faceless brick apartment building across the street. The room was closetless, was furnished with a narrow bed, a wardrobe permanently ajar, a mahogany-veneer dresser and a small chintz-covered stuffed chair. An additional chair might be supplied, she said, if the tenant required more than one. There was a bathroom down the hall he might want to inspect, which had a new plumbing system.

"How much?" he asked.

She showed him the bathroom and another room on the floor, which she referred to as a kitchen, a closet-sized space with a two burner hotplate and a refrigerator slightly larger than a bread box.

"Twenty pounds a week including continental breakfast," she said.

"How much is it without breakfast?" he asked.

The question distressed her, caused her eyes to narrow and her shoulders to quiver under an invisible weight. "It's the same," she said, "with or without the breakfast. If you looked around, I'm sure you noticed that you can't do any better than what I'm asking."

Tom went into his pants pocket and took out a twenty pound note. "I don't know how long I'll be staying," he said.

"You can move in anytime," the woman said, folding the twenty pound bill in thirds and putting it in the pocket of her housedress. "I don't care what you do in that room as long as everything is kept in the same condition you find it. I've made an inventory of each and every item in your care."

He went back into the room to see if his memory of it had survived the passage of fifteen minutes. When you approached it without expectation of grace or charm or comfort, the room wasn't bad at all. The landlady waited for him in the hall, her demeanor faintly ironic as if she knew some minor fraud were being perpetrated on one or both sides.

"I suppose you'd like a receipt," she said as if the request (he hadn't made) was the first excess of many she might expect from him.

He wouldn't have been surprised if she had propositioned him in the next breath, or accused him of coming on to her with lecherous intent. If she weren't watching him, he might have stashed the gun in one of the dresser drawers, its insistent weight burdening his hip. Guarding the door like a jailer, she asked him again if it would please him to have a receipt.

He said, joining her in the hall, that the room was exactly what he wanted and he would move in that evening.

The receipt, written in illegible hand, was on a half-sheet of letterhead, the landlady's name and address printed at the top. O. Chepstow, Fashion Specialist. 62 Wornington Road. London W2.

Tom was outside and halfway down the block when he realized he hadn't gotten a key. Embarrassed at having to come back, he hesitated at the door, his finger in the air. The imposing figure of O. Chepstow appeared just as he pressed the buzzer or even perhaps an instant before. She held out an open hand, two keys in her massive palm, as if she were feeding a skittish horse. "I knew you'd come back," she said.

"I couldn't keep away," he said, mirroring her grim smile.

When you thought of one thing leading to another, this was the other led to by the first. Tom had gone into a W.H. Smith's with the idea of getting himself a notebook in which to keep a journal, an activity urged on him by his mother. When he left the store he had handguns in both jacket pockets, the second a toy that bore the real one a more than generic resemblance. Impressed with the toy's verisimilitude, he had put it in his left hand pocket as counter ballast to the other. Since the toy gun was nothing he wanted, nothing he had planned to buy, nothing he had even conceived a use for, he walked out without acknowledging the acquisition. He edged away from the store with his head down, keeping an even pace, expecting someone to come running up behind him calling "Thief." His expectation unfulfilled, he spoke the word to himself, became his own accuser. The moment he felt free of pursuit, his exhilaration died. He walked around London for the rest of the afternoon, picking up odds and ends, escaping retribution, until it was almost dark. Then, after a series of phone calls, he slipped into his father's house, repossessed his suitcase, and moved, body and baggage, into his new home.

3

Lukas Terman was in his study, obsessing over a line of dialogue, when the phone provided a not altogether welcome interruption.

"I'm disturbed with something you've done," Isabelle announced in a bristling voice.

He couldn't imagine what it was, thought his recent behavior beyond reproach. "I've been growing old, Isabelle, waiting for you to return," he said. He felt himself aging as he spoke the line.

"Not true, is it, that you accepted an invitation for us to go to Kent for the weekend? You don't think you might have consulted me, Terman? Is there something about me, my line of work perhaps, that makes you think I'm incapable of making decisions for myself?"

Her exaggerated outrage seemed out of character and Terman assumed she was still angry at him for having asked her to leave. "If you don't want to go, we won't go," he said. "I've always had the greatest respect for your decision-making capacity."

"Max said you had committed us to this visit."

"Max was making trouble," he said. "It's how he keeps his hand in when he's not working on a film." He found himself in the throes of a rage that subsided as abruptly and mystifyingly as it arose. "Sweetheart, why don't we continue this fight in person?"

"Sweetheart yourself," she said in a softer voice. "You know, Terman, it might be fun to have a weekend in the country, don't you think? I'd rather like to go if you can manage it."

"Let's talk about it when you come over, Isabelle. We could all go out for a meal at Tethers or at that wine pub in Ladbroke Grove. Tom ought to be awake by then and if he's not I'll shake him out of bed. I haven't eaten anything all day."

"Terman," she said, squeezing the name as if it were one long syllable, "just a bit ago I got a call from Tom. He told me he's rented a

Bed and Breakfast somewhere on the outskirts of Notting Hill Gate. Tom's not in the house, is he?"

He went upstairs to look into Tom's room, then returned to the phone to acknowledge his inexplicable mistake. He had somehow assumed when Tom hadn't shown himself that the boy was asleep in his room. The illusion of Tom's presence gone, the house felt emptier than before. Isabelle said that she would come over to talk—the word talk emphasized—if he felt in need of company but she wanted it clear that she wasn't going to spend the night. Terman said even if he were unforgivable, he thought that she'd have the grace to forgive him. The issue of her staying was left unresolved.

"I have the feeling you're angry with me," she said.

In the scene he had been reworking, he had left Henry Berger in a phone booth, though as he came back to it he was unable to determine the occasion. It troubled him only a little, this failure of memory, as if something in his own life he wanted to shake off.

Berger was on the phone to Colonel Saracen, requesting a face to face interview (though that may have been a different time).

Saracen: It's good to hear your voice, boyo. Rumor had it that you had permanently lost your way.

Berger: Could you meet me at the warehouse in Barking, Colonel, in, say twenty minutes. I have that information you've been after.

Saracen: Can't possibly make it. Not possible. Where are you calling from, Henry?

Berger: Yes, well, I thought what I had might interest you.

Saracen: I hope you haven't mentioned this to anyone else, boyo. I can meet you in an hour, if that's the only way.

Berger: Thirty minutes, Colonel. (Berger hangs up, dials another number.) Is Major Lindstrom there?

Cut to Henry Berger entering the warehouse building he had been imprisoned in earler, Berger lookng behind him as he steps inside.

We cut to a figure in an Austin Healey putting on purple gloves with fastidious preoccupation, his face obscured.

Two figures approach the warehouse from opposing directions, enter warily the almost pitch black building. Berger waits until they are both in the room, then turns on the overhead spotlights. The camera moves between triangulated shadows.

Berger: I have a fix on both of you.

Camera follows Saracen as he moves slowly out of the shadows, his hands out of sight.

Berger: You too, Major.

Saracen: So it's you, old friend. Double agent, is it?

Lindstrom moves a step or so forward from his corner, only the front of him illuminated, his face still in shadow.

Berger: One more step, Major. I want to see your hands. If you don't throw your gun on the floor in front of you and step into the light, I'm going to have to kill you.

Lindstrom: For God's sake, Berger, use your head. Saracen set this charade up so that he might get both of us out of the way.

Berger: Is that the truth, Colonel?

Saracen: What do you want me to say, Henry? If you can't trust me, who can you trust? I've suspected Lindstrom from day one.

Lindstrom: Ask Colonel Saracen about the Walmer Connection.

Berger moves the point of his gun from Lindstrom to Saracen, from Saracen to Lindstrom.

Shot of Lindstrom's face through the sights of Berger's pistol, the mouth the target of focus.

Saracen (shouting): He's going for his gun. Put him away.

We see a purple-gloved hand reaching for a gun, followed by the sound of a shot. There are two further shots and the man in the purple gloves—we are still not clear who it is—falls.

Lindstrom: Had me a little worried there, Berger. Have to admit. How did you figure Saracen was the man?

Berger: (his ear to Saracen's chest, turns suddenly to see Lindstrom, hand in pocket, watching him): It figured, didn't it, that it was one of you.

"Don't you write any real books anymore?" he imagines Tom asking him.

"As a matter of fact," Terman says. "I have a draft of a new novel in the bottom of this desk. Is that what you mean by real books?"

#

Henry Berger and Colonel Saracen meet as if accidentally at Waterloo Bridge. A light rain falling, a mist of rain.

Saracen: Seven men—seven at least that we know of—met once a week in a two room flat on Belsize Park Road in Folkestone. All of them except one were distinguished men in their respective fields. We have some idea why they met and what their ties were to one another. Five of these men have died unnatural deaths. It stands to reason that one of the two (or three) survivors—there may have been an eighth member of the society—is the killer of the others and that the remaining survivor or suvivors is in immediate danger.

Berger: Two other men have died who have no connection to that secret society and apparently at the hand of the same killer or killers. How does that work into your theory, Colonel?

Saracen: They knew too much or got in the way. Irrelevancies, boyo. My money is on our French nobleman, André Lange, alias Pierre de Chartres, the man in the dark raincoat you saw running away in the catacombs. Lay your hands on him, boyo, and we can all take a vacation in the sun.
Berger: And what about the seventh man?
Saracen: Inspector D'Agostino, retired police officer. Legs impaired. Has a bodyguard at his side night and day. Not likely. Not bloody likely. Be a dear boy and bring in Monsieur Lange.

#

He thought he heard the key turning in the lock, the slightest noise reverberating in the large house. If someone were coming in, he would hear the door open and shut like a muffled cough. If it were Isabelle, she would make her presence known almost immediately, calling to him from the base of the stairs.

Although he heard no further sounds, Terman came out of his study and hurried down the carpeted stairs, aware of the thump of his own step as if it were coming from somewhere else. No one was in the front room waiting for him. He opened the door to look outside and saw Isabelle coming up the walk. His silhouette, larger than life, waited for her in the doorway.

"You frightened me," she said when she saw he was there.

It was only afterward, after he had persuaded her to go to bed, after they had made love in a desultory way, imitating the gestures of former passion, that he asked her if she had been at the door with her key five or ten minutes before he actually saw her.

The question, he could tell, offended her, though she made no more of it than necessary. He trusted her denial and assumed that he had imagined the sound—such a small sound anyway—of someone turning a key in a lock. It came to him later on that if someone had let himself in, he(whoever) was still skulking somewhere in the house.

Terman slept fitfully, heard from time to time some unaccountable movement in the house, recorded almost every unseen tremor.

Isabelle woke in a irritable mood, accused him of contriving at every turn to defeat her. They had a brief fight which resolved itself in silences. Terman accompanied her to her flat after breakfast, despite her assertion that she preferred to go alone. When they got to her place, she apologized and invited him in and they pressed against each other savagely though fully clothed, then Terman went home, though not before asking her if she had Tom's address. She said no, that she knew the street but not the number, knew the phone number but not the address, which he suspected was a lie. "I care for you," she called after him. "Don't you know that?"

#

The phone rang any number of times that first evening at the Kirstner's cottage in Ramsgate, but the call was never the one Terman was waiting for.

"The trouble with you Americans," Max was saying to an audience, "and it's great worry to us all, is that you're so bloody child-centered. In Britain, we set the babies an example—we send them to boarding school until they're beaten into ploughshares."

"He's not even English," Marjorie said to no one in particular.

Terman had two glasses of red wine in front of him, clarets of rival claim, one half-filled, the other as yet untouched. Max opened another bottle he wanted Terman to try, a '74 Graves from an obscure chateau and set a third glass in front of him. Isabelle had her hand on his arm, a temporary restraint.

At some point Isabelle got up and moved to another part of the room, provoked at something he had said or done, an unwitting transgression. A prematurely white-haired man, who had money or was a source of money (he'd forgotten what Max had said about him), occupied Isabelle's place on the couch next to him. It was the man, who, at Max's office, had announced himself as an admirer.

"This seat's already spoken for," Terman said. "I'm afraid you'll have to find one of your own."

The man, who looked like a youngish Wilfred Hyde White, smiled broadly. "It is, is it?" he said. "Well, I'll just keep it warm until the young lady returns. Name's Tumson, point of fact. Edward Tumsun."

"Your reputation trails you like a shadow, Tumsun,"he said in a loud voice, winking at Marjorie Kirstner who was sitting across from him.

Tumsun took a business card from his wallet and slipped it into the breast pocket of Terman's jacket. "I'll let my card speak for me," he said.

That Tumsun presumed to invade his space irritated him beyond reason. "So you have a talking card?" he said. "Does it speak in tongues?" He noticed the director watching him from across the room, framing the scene. "Does it speak the language of money?"

"Hard cash," said Tumsun.

"I have the idea that the card's the ventriloquist,"he said, "and you're just pretending it's the other way around."

"I wouldn't advise making an enemy of me," Tumsun said, getting up, his unshakable smile etched into his face.

Isabelle came over a few minutes after Tumsun had vacated the seat. "You're not still sulking about Tom, are you?" she asked.

"I'm tasting wines," he said. He engaged the three glasses on the glass table in front of him, each in its turn.

She sat down next to him and put her arm around his shoulders. "I'm sorry you feel so awful," she whispered. "If Tom needs you, he'll get in touch."

He kissed her ear. "Let's go upstairs to one of the bedrooms."

"You're mad," she said.

Max came by and filled one of his empty glasses with a '67 Burgundy that he guaranteed would knock him on his ear. "What did you and Tumsun talk about?" he asked out of the side of his mouth.

"He let his card do his talking," Terman said in a voice that seemed to extend itself into every corner of the room. "The language it talked of was not one of mine."

Max gave him a severe look. "That card talks everyone's language," he said. "It is universally articulate. Not advisable to make an enemy of the man."

"He said the same thing."

He noticed that Max looked elsewhere while talking to him, seemed to be counting the house.

"Are we going upstairs or not?" he asked Isabelle when Max was gone. Everything irritated him.

"We really can't, can we?" she said. "It would be so rude." She turned her face away.

He sipped the Burgundy with no sense of its distinction, rued his failure to make connection. "If you won't go with me, I'll go alone," he said.

On the way to the bathroom, moving through a narrow hallway, a twilight landscape of betrayal and deception, he bumped into a marble sculpture, dislodging it from its pedestal with his shoulder. A chip split off on contact with the floor, a large earlike shape. He lifted the ambiguous sculpture (a woman with her head seemingly between her legs, hair streaming), wrestled it onto its pedestal, but had no success in disguising the statue's wound. Each time he replaced the broken fragment, it would slip loose again. Marjorie passed him in the hall, said she was going to sleep, then stayed on to observe his efforts.

At some point she took the broken piece from him and pressed it successfully in its place. "You were holding it the wrong way," she told him.

"I'll pay for the damage," he said.

A big-boned, athletic woman, horsy-handsome in the English fashion, she winked at him. "It's our secret," she said, leaving him.

Terman let himself into the bathroom and locked the door. His face was out of focus in the mirror, eyes like worm holes in an apple. He held his prick in his hand like a marksman and fired point blank into the void. While he peed in endless profusion, he thought he heard the phone ring and he held fire until the ringing stopped. It was not that he wanted to hear from Tom but that he felt he ought to want to hear. No one called him to the phone. His burden slipped away, vanished unexpectedly, then returned.

#

Terman woke during the night, tumbled from dreams into blackness. A sharp thought like a bramble pricked him. The only thing to do was to go back to London and collect his son. He climbed out of bed and dressed himself blindly in yesterday's clothes. Isabelle raised her head, said something the matter? Nothing, he said.

He tiptoed down the unfamiliar stairs, the house silent and dark, invested in shadows. There was a light on in the kitchen, calling attention to itself. He pushed open the door and looked in. Marjorie was sitting at the table, wearing a man's silk dressing gown, the sleeves rolled up. "I'm going back to London to get something," "What a bore!" she said, putting her head down on the table. He had the idea she had been crying and closed the door behind him, was closing it when she called his name in a world-weary voice.

"Do you have a cig?" she asked.

"No," he said.

"What good are you?"

There was a car parked directly behind his in the driveway and his first inclination was to see fate as his implacable opponent and return to bed. Even as he opened the door of Tumsun's Bentley and released the handbrake, he could imagine Marjorie saying with that casual contempt that seemed bred into the voice, "You're back, are you, even before you started." The car obstructing his path was difficult to move, adamant about its right of place. He threw his shoulder repeatedly against the left fender, rolling the car back a few feet at a time. Whenever he stopped to catch his breath, the Bentley tended to slip forward. Someone, he sensed, was watching him from the house, taking pleasure in the extravagance of his effort.

He breathed rage. A cold hour passed before there was room for him to get out and by then he was shivering from the exertion, hot and cold at the same time, his face glazed with sweat. Once he was on the road, the trip, despite the veils of fog, seemed to make itself. He was back in London with the first light, parking across the street from his house. He noticed even before he parked the car that there was a light on in one of the third floor windows. His idea was that Tom had come back, had moved back in his absence.

The light was coming from Tom's room, but the room was untenanted, showed no signs of having been otherwise employed. Terman didn't recall leaving the light on, was all but positive he hadn't, which meant that Tom (or someone else) had visited the room briefly. He lay down on the bed and closed his eyes, tested the bed, woke as he saw something rush from the closet toward him. He sat up in the bed in an empty room, the overhead light glaring. He turned the light off before leaving, recalled to himself the act of pushing the wall switch down with the index finger of his right hand.

He fixed himself a cup of instant coffee, though he had no taste for it once made and poured it down the sink. What did his son want from him? "Tom," he shouted from the bottom of the stairwell. "Are you there?" His voice rattled the walls. "Where the hell are you?" He expected no acknowledgement of his cry and was fulfilled in that expectation alone.

He went to his study to check something in an early draft of *The Folkstone Conspiracies*—then called *The Last Days of Civilization*—found himself turning out the drawers of his desk, looking for something else. The gun wasn't where he remembered putting it and he persuaded himself, not wanting to believe it had been stolen, that he had absent-mindedly moved it to another place. Where else might he have put it, wanting it at the same time out of sight and at hand?

He went through every drawer in the desk, systematically emptying and refilling, searching for the gun as if it were an object half its size. The box of ammunition was also missing. He had left Ramsgate in the dead hours of the night, paralyzed by exhaustion to discover that Tom had stolen a gun from his desk. There was some comfort in having his most disheartening suspicions borne out.

#

Returning from Europa Foods with a bag of croissants, two oranges, and a bottle of white wine, Terman rang his own bell before letting himself in with the key. The mail had been delivered through the slot; otherwise the house was as he remembered leaving it, though also different, changed by time, by modifications in the patterns of light and shade, by the actuality or potentiality of another presence. There was a letter from Magda, one from his agent in New York that included a check he had been expecting, and one, written on American Express stationery, that he suspected was from Tom. It was already nine o'clock (actually two minutes to nine) and he dialed Ramsgate to tell Max he was on his way back. Marjorie answered, said Max was still sleeping, but that she expected him up and about any time now. "What are you doing in London?" she asked.

"Looking for a gun," he said.

"How positively bloody-minded of you! I hope you didn't make anything of last night. I'm the kind of person who can do without sleep altogether if it comes to that."

"An enviable quality,"he said.

"Hurry back to us," she said.

Terman returned to his study and took one final turn through the drawers in his desk. The news was inescapably the same. He composed a note to Tom, demanding the return of the gun, then tore it up and dropped the scraps in the wastebasket. Someone else might have taken the gun—others had keys to the house—or he might have displaced the gun himself out of distraction. As he was going down the stairs he had an image of Tom sitting on the floor of his study piecing the note together.

Terman nodded off for prolonged stretches, waking to find himself straddling two lanes, a horn trumpeting in the background.

He pulled off the Motorway first chance he had, parked the car with the object of taking a nap, then he remembered the letter from his son and opened that instead. He wondered why he had waited so long to deal with it.

He screened his eyes as he read as if to avoid the direct rays of the sun. There was no mention in the letter of the missing gun, no direct mention. The letter started out as an apology, and ended up as a bill of grievances. There was nothing new except an edginess in tone and with it an air of undefined threat. The letter was typed on an electric typwriter with the same or similar typeface as the one he had in his study in the Holland Park house. Was that the real message,the implicit confesson of intrusion and theft? He sensed that there was something else in the letter beneath the litany of complaints ("Whenever we're together you act as if you wish you were somewhere else."), an unspecified request, an asking for something while refusing to ask.

Isabelle greeted him with a kiss, running from the house to embrace him. "I missed you," she said lightly.

"I've missed myself,"he said. "Has Max been wanting to get to work?"

"Max took most of his entourage to see the Dover Castle. He asked if you and I wanted to go and I said no. I don't believe he even knew you had gone off."

"Did I get any calls?"he asked.

"Someone rang up this morning while we were all having breakfast and then hung up without speaking a word. If you want that one, you can have it."

Terman went into one of the back rooms on the first floor and in a little over an hour rewrote a scene that had been troubling Max. The house was empty when he finished work and after taking a plum from the refrigerator he went out for a walk. He wondered if he should lock the outside door and didn't.

He walked along the water's edge, had the illusion, looking into the fog that veiled the French coast, that he had gone as far as he could go. After awhile, tired of his own company, he sat down on a bench near the strand and took his son's letter from the breast pocket of his jacket. He was about to reread it when he heard his name in the air, saw himself frozen inescapably in the sights of his caller.

The recitation of his name startled him. When he looked up he expected to see a gun pointed in his face.

"I saw a child drown," Isabelle said.

It seemed like an odd thing for her to say to him and he looked up from his letter with a bemused grin.

"Terman, for pity's sake!" Her voice trilled. "A child, three, four years old, was drowned in the channel. I saw a man walk into the water with his clothes on and carry out this lifeless little creature." She pointed down the beach toward where a crowd had formed.

The news made its way—his distraction so great—as if it had been beamed across the channel into France and back again. "A child was drowned?" The question was rhetorical.

She felt compelled to tell the story to him from beginning to end.

"You tell it very well," he said.

"It's so terrible, isn't it?"

He put his arm on her shoulder and they walked back to the Kirstners' house, circumventing the crowd of mourners. It worried him that he felt nothing for the child, imagining it by turns as his own or as himself.

"They'll hate themselves, won't they?" she said. "I can't imagine a marriage surviving something dreadful like that. They'll take to blaming each other, don't you think."

The image of the child face down in the water kept him company, the child embryonic, the water like amniotic fluid. He held the oppressive image before him, suffocating in the water himself yet unable to feel the slightest compassion.

When they were back at the house he showed her his son's letter.

"What do you make of it?" he asked when she returned it to him without a word.

"There's the obvious thing,"she said. "And beyond that I couldn't even begin to guess."

He took back the letter, reinserted it in its envelope and returned it to his jacket pocket. "What's the obvious thing?" he asked.

She gave him one of her narrow-eyed glances and slipped out of the room. "I thought school was out," he imagined her saying.

Terman fell asleep over the *Observer,* lost the world for the briefest of interludes. When he woke up Max Kirstner and the others were back. Isabelle had gone off somewhere,had left him as he dozed, their conversation stuck in the broken teeth of some obscure misunderstanding.

When he opened his eyes he had the sense that he had been immersed in water for a dangerously long time.

Kirstner and Tumsun and another man, an international actor with an impassive boyish face, a man who gave the impression in his films of being raptured with self-admiration, were talking in French. Marjorie and a woman named Sylvie, an actress who had come with Tumsun,were in the kitchen, confiding in echoing whispers over preparations for lunch.

His presumptive conspirator took him aside at first opportunity. "I'd like your opinion of Emile as Henry Berger. He's not absolutely right, though he has a certain quality that's in the script. The suspicion of irony in even his most sincere gestures."

"And the suspicion of sincerity in even his most ironic gestures."

Kirstner pulled him over into a corner, one eye on the others as he talked. "You need anything?" he asked. "You all right?"

"When someone asks me if I'm all right," Terman said, "It's gererally because he's doing something to make me feel not all right. What are you doing to me, Max?"

Max apologized exaggeratedly for having ignored him, said he hoped that Terman could manage without him in the afternoon as he promised to show Emile and some others the local color, a chore (he assured him by pursung his lips) he would prefer to avoid. "You'll be all right?" he asked, his arm on Terman's shoulder. "Of course you will be."

"Of course I will be," Terman said.

They had lunch in the garden—oysters, baked ham, paté, cheese and white wine—Emile insisted on drinking bourbon—and sat until it was almost four o'clock.

When Max got into his car to show Emile the sights the afternoon was fading into retrospect. Marjorie and Sylvie elected to sunbathe in the enclosed garden, to make use of what remained of the hot sun. Tumsum thought of going along for the ride—he had already had the tour once—but decided to take a nap instead. Isabelle couldn't decide what she wanted to do, said she would take a ride into town with Max if he was going past the shops. Terman, not asked to come along, went into the workroom to look over the scene he had written earlier in the day.

He was composing an answer to Tom's letter when he was interrupted by a knock at the door.

"Come in," he called. When he stood up he could see the sunbathers in the garden from his window. There was no response to his invitation, and the knock, if that's what it was, had not repeated itself. He considered throwing the door open, though instead moved closer to the window to glance at the two women in the garden. They each wore only the bottom half of a bikini, and Terman, not ordinarily a voyeur, appraised them from the window. They lay at right angles, or almost right angles, head to cheek, forming a bent L, Marjorie on her back, Sylvie, who seemed a miniature of the other, on her side. He imagined himself embraced between them.

"Who is it?" he called, turning his head away from the garden.

He returned to the safety of his typewriter, found himself waiting for a second knock at the door. He was unaccountably out of breath, disturbed by the failure of events to define themselves. "Why can't you just accept me as I am?" he wrote to his son.

#

Henry Berger wakes to find himself strapped to a bed in a small punitively antiseptic hospital room. After a moment, a woman in a nurse's uniform comes in and locks the door behind her.

Nurse: My name is Adamantha. I'll be looking after you until you're well again, sir. If there's anything I can do to make your stay with us more pleasurable, I would like to know what it is.

Berger: I'd be obliged, sweetheart, if you unstrapped my hands.

Adamantha: Are the straps too tight, sir?

Berger: Too tight? Yes.

Adamantha: I can't help you there, I'm afraid. Only Dr. X has the authority to remove the straps. They are there, do I need to tell you, for your own good.

Berger: You can do anything for me but remove the straps. Is that right?

Adamantha wheels a tray of food over to the bed.

Adamantha: I'll be your hands for you, sir. I'll give you nothing to complain of, I promise. Would you like your lunch or would you like to have your massage first?

Berger: What's supposed to be wrong with me?

Adamantha: You'll have to ask the doctor that, won't you?

Berger: What do you call this place?

She offers to feed him what seems to be a bowl of soup; he turns his head away, refusing to eat.

Adamantha (opening the top few buttons of her uniform): If not food, sir, what is it that will content you?

Berger: I want to know where I am. I want the straps removed from my wrists. I want to know what's wrong with me.

Adamantha (looking at her watch): The doctor will be back in precisely twelve minutes, sir. He knows everything about your case. I am here, I say this unofficially, to ease your burdens in any way I can.

We cut away from Henry Berger to the small window—a glimpse of sky, an outline of fields and mountain as insubstantial as a backdrop, a view of anonymous undefined landscape. Slowly the camera pans back to the hospital bed, discovers Adamantha on top of Henry Berger, riding him, whispering endearments. Berger, who is still strapped to the bed, offers only limited response. Adamantha seems a whirlwind of energy.

Momentarily, we see the room through Henry Berger's eyes. There is a ceiling fan turning slowly, a fly buzzing at the window, the nurse's face distorted luxuriantly with pleasure or anguish, the window, a row of three wood chairs against a wall, a framed print of a topographical map, scars in the light blue wall, gouges as if someone had tried to break through with a blunt instrument, the window again, the faded sky, the fan turning slowly, the door. The door opens slightly—a figure remains in shadow, is unrevealed—then closes again.

Berger: What was that?

Adamantha (in a lulling whisper): There was nothing, nothing. You must learn not to jump at mere noises. It uses your body up in tension, tires one to death. Oh how weary it is to be always on your guard, jumping at shadows. Suspicion confirms itself, you know. There have been case studies. There is no one to be afraid of here, no danger, no threat to your security. You are safe as a baby with us, absolutely safe, perfectly safe.

Berger: I want to get out of here.

Adamantha: Do not interrupt me. Have you no respect? Without trust, there is no safety. Isn't it trust what's wanted? Isn't it just that? You've never trusted a soul, have you? You can't, you don't know how, have never learned the secret of trust. You want to trust me but something in you, something ugly and unnecessary, something diseased at the heart, says watch out. Watching out has never gotten you anywhere, has it? Now close your eyes and think of trust, think only of trust. Give yourself to trust.

Berger (closing his eyes): Take off the straps.

Adamantha (riding him backwards): Soon they will come off, very soon. We are here to take care of you, to see that you come to no harm. You must trust that.

Berger (weakly): Please take them off. My wrists hurt.

Adamantha: I will take them off in no time at all. As soon as you are ready. Yes?

We cut to the door, watch it expectantly, then pan along the wall to the window and then to the ceiling (the fan revolving so slowly that its movement seems almost a trick of the eye) and then abruptly to the bed, the room tipping, spilling itself. Berger is on top of Adamantha now, has her on her stomach, arms and legs pinned.

The door opens and a white-haired man steps in.

Dr. X: And how is our patient coming along?

Berger, stark naked, springs on him from behind the door, holding him in a hammer-lock around the neck.

Berger: If you cry out, I'll break you neck.

Dr. X: You are making an unfortunate mistake, Mr. Berger. We are your friends here.

Berger: Do you always strap your friends to the bed? Is that your idea of hospitality?

Dr. X: Truly it was for your own safety. You had taken a powerful hallucinatory drug and I was afraid you might do yourself some danger. Yes?

Berger: Were you afraid for my life?

Dr. X: Henry, I feel as if you were my own son. This is the truth. The drug you have taken stays in the blood stream in a dormant fashion, taking effect without warning—it is so new its effects are barely understood—so that from one moment to the next your whole personality may change. If an antidote isn't administered in a week—two weeks at most—it is possible that you will enter a psychotic phase from which there is no return.

Berger (tightening his grip): Where have you put my clothes?

Dr. X: I... can't... breathe. Please, I will take you to them.

Berger is dressed and going through the pockets of his jacket. The doctor is trussed to his desk chair, a bandage taped over his mouth.

Berger (removing one end of the bandage): My gun and passport are missing. What did you do with them?

Dr. X: There is no gun when you are brought in. That is the truth. Your passport is in the bottom drawer of my desk. Can't you see that I am your friend, Henry? It may even be that I am your real... (*Berger retapes the bandage over his mouth, goes through the drawers of the doctor's desk.*)

4

Eyes down, shoulders slumped forward as though to make himself less conspicuous, Tom goes to 27 Foxglove Road to visit Astrid and her convalescent father. Her dad has been quite a trial since returning from hospital, Astrid has confided. The blows on the head have left him with only patches of memory and even those were not wholly to be trusted. There were mornings when he didn't recognize his own daughter. In the beginning it had made her cry but she had learned to deal with it, or if not quite that, had come to accept his periodic blankness as a temporary disorder. With her dad unable to work, there was little money coming in, next to nothing. And her dad couldn't be left alone, was prone to violent, heart-stopping fears, Astrid required to look after him day and night. Or if not Astrid, someone else. A friend named Mary Flaherty came over to sit with him while Astrid worked three days a week at American Express on Regents Street.

They were having tea in the parlor, Tom and Astrid, when the father bawled "Asty" from the room next door. Astrid looked into his room to see what he needed.

"Who the hell is that strange boy?" he asked.

"Da, that's the American boy," she said softly. "His name is Tommy."

"I don't recall having had that pleasure," he said. "You can tell me over and again that I've met the lad but I can't believe something for which I have no experience, can I?" For the third time (or fourth), Astrid presented Tom to her father. He shook Tom's hand, said, "Heard so much about you, Tom, I feel like I know you already. Astrid, I suppose, has told you of our situation. We don't do so badly, the two of us. Wouldn't you say so, Asty?"

"You do," she said with mournful insistence, "very, very well."

"I'm not the one to sit idly by and be pampered," he said to no one in particular. "That's the worst of it. The best of it is having Asty about to give me a hand." He held on to his daughter's hand like a lover.

"He self-dramatizes," she said to Tom when they were alone. They sat in the parlor, talking in hushed voices while the father watched television on the other side of the door. The shabby sitting room diminished with increasing acquaintance, seemed barely larger than the space taken up by its two occupants.

The conditions of Astrid's life, the combination of misfortunes, moved Tom to a kind of passion. "I'd like to take you away from all this," he said, the joke a disguise for something genuinely felt.

"You're going to take me away from it all, are you?" she said, averting her face.

It was not as if he thought her beautiful or sexy or scintillatingly intelligent, though he aspired to discover one or another of these qualities in her. It was not even that she loved him or found his company amusing or reassuring, or offered him, even for a moment, some gratifying illusion.

"Do you think you could go out with me some time?" he asked.

Her brow knitted. "I don't really know what you have in mind."

He had nothing in mind beyond a further statment of what he might do for her if she would only let him. "We could to a movie or go out for dinner or rob a bank," he said.

She didn't laugh, was not easily amused, which was the thing about her that fascinated him most, her relentless, unassuming, weightless gravity.

He got up dutifully to go. "I'll be back," he said after they had shaken hands.

She brushed her straw-colored hair from her eyes, said goodbye with measured indifference, all her energy committed to a flutter of embarrassment.

#

He was writing a letter to his mother, inventing the details of his stay in London (creating himself a as a character he might sympathize with), when the ubiquitous Mrs. Chepstow knocked at his door, her face preceding the knock by a fraction of a second. His father had called, she said. She presented him with a half sheet of letterhead that had an out-of-city phone number printed on it in childish hand.

O. Chepstow watched him descend the steps from the doorway of her apartment. "You're asked to ring back immediately," she said as he passed.

Tom thanked her for the message, said he would make the call at first opportunity.

#

Astrid opened the door in slow motion, squinted at him, perplexed by the light.

"You said to come over on Saturday," he reminded her.

She nodded, though seemed to have no recollection of any such invitation. "My da had a bad night," she said. "He woke up around two in the morning with the impression that he was supposed to be at work. He put his clothes on over his pajamas and, in his super hurry, he fell down half a flight of stairs. We thought he might have to go to hospital."

"That's terrible," Tom said.

They sat apart on the vinyl couch in the foyer in which they almost always spent their time together.

"How is he?" he asked. "Is he at home?"

Astrid looked up, smiled wanly, her eyes bloodshot from lack of sleep. "Did you say something? I was in a bit of a reverie."

"I'm sorry," he said.

"It's not your fault."

The conversation tended to die between them, and Tom felt dismissed by her silence, sought out a gesture that might reclaim his call on her attention. "You know I'd like to help you," he said.

Astrid was staring at her hands. "I don't know what you mean," she said. "What can you possibly do for me?" Despite the complaint in her tone, he could tell she was pleased.

He thought of taking his father's gun from his pocket and showing it to her.

"What did you have in mind?" she asked.

"Forget it," he said.

"No, tell me."

He let her lean forward before he answered and even then he hesitated, drawing her out, sharpening expectation. He mumbled, embarrassed by the crudeness of his offer, that he might be able to lay his hands on some money.

She seemed scandalized by his offer, by the weight of its temptation.

"What would you think of me, Tommy, if I took money from you?" She put her hand on his arm, then quickly drew it back.

He offered a secretive smile in answer, felt for the first time in her presence a small breath of desire, an unanticipated wind from the south.

Astrid got up from the couch and looked into her father's bedroom. "He's sleeping the sleep of the blessed," she whispered, her finger over her lips. When she returned to the couch she sat with her leg pressed against his.

His suggestion that they go for a walk was not premeditated, was impelled by the urgency of the moment. He had to get some air, he thought, or he would go out of his mind.

She didn't answer, seemed puzzled by his request. "Is it all right if I smoke?" she asked.

What he wanted was more air, not less. "You don't want to go for a walk or you don't want to leave your father even for a few minutes?"

She dug into her purse for a pack of mentholated cigarettes. "It's all right here, isn't it? I mean it's not grand, but it's all right."

"I wasn't putting down your place," he said. "It's one of my favorite places outside the continental United States. I particularly like sitting on this couch."

"I think you'd really rather go for a walk. Isn't that so?" She took his hand, swung it briefly then turned it loose. "What is this passion for walking, Tommy?"

"What is this passion for sitting still, lady?" He stood up, made restless by the idea of sitting.

The phone rang and she took it in her room with the door closed.

The brief interlude seemed to revive her spirits. She was determinedly flirtatious on her return, offered him nothing beyond the transparent insincerity of her performance. "If you really want to do me a favor, Tommy," she whispered, "you know what you could do?"

"What could I do?"

She smoked as if it were a form of nourishment, closed her eyes as she took sustenance. "I don't think it right of me to ask," she said.

"I'll do whatever you want."

She thought about it, tortured herself with indecision. "Would you"—she hesitated—"stay with my father this afternoon? Mary was supposed to come by but she had to do something else."

He said okay, thought to ask where she was going.

She gave him his instructions and kissed him on the cheek, a sudden blossom of energy. "I appreciate this so much," she said, putting on her coat. In a moment she was gone.

Left to himself, he looked into Astrid's room which he had never been invited to inspect. Except for a pair of flowered panties at the foot of the bed, the room was as tidy and impersonal as a monk's cell. He sat on her bed, browsed in her meager library, studied the photos on her dresser top. Her life seemed pathetic and ordinary, even beyond what he had imagined, though he assumed the evidence was incomplete.

He used Astrid's phone to dial the number on the sheet of paper the landlady had given him. After the second ring he changed his mind and hung up.

The old man, as he thought of him, was calling for something or hallucinating in his sleep. "I'm coming," Tom said. There was no sound after that, not even the sterterous breathing that came periodically from behind the closed door. Tom peeked through a crack and saw Astrid's father standing warily behind the door with a shoe in his hand as a weapon. "It's the American boy, Tom," he said. "Astrid's friend, Tom."

#

When Tom got to the Green Park tube stop, Astrid was already there, looking for him in the wrong direction.

She seemed out of breath. "I thought I was the one that would be late," she said.

As they walked into the park, she glanced repeatedly over her shoulder, wary of some invisible pursuer.

There wasn't an empty bench and he suggested sitting in the grass.

I'm not dressed for it," she said. "We could just walk about if you don't mind."

He took off his field jacket, forgetting that the gun was in one of the pockets, and spread it out on the ground.

"What's that for?" she asked, her voice rising plaintively. "That won't keep my dress from being squooshed, will it?"

"You'll be careful," he said. "You're a very careful person."

His remark creased her face like a shadow or a slap. He sat down first, then she sat.

"It's not comfortable," she said, getting to her feet. She brushed the offending touch of his jacket from the back of her skirt.

He remembered the gun, made certain it was still in his pocket before getting up.

"What time do you have?" she asked.

"Don't worry about the time, okay? This is actually the first opportunity we've had to talk without your father in the next room."

She lifted his wrist to look at his watch, studied it a moment with vacant intensity. "It's not going, is it? How am I supposed to know when to get back."

He shook his arm with clownish fervor until the watch took heart. After they had walked another five minutes he took a silk scarf from his jacket pocket and slipped it into her hand.

She held it without looking at it. "It's a Liberty's, isn't it?"

"Whatever," he said. "Liberty's. Tyranny's. It's for you if you want it."

She seemed burdened by the gift, though also mildly exhilarated. She kissed him on both cheeks. "That's the way they show their appreciation in France," she said.

"How do they do it in England?" he asked.

Once they were out of the park she became fidgety again. "I should get back to work, shouldn't I?"

He walked her past Buckingham Palace toward Trafalgar Square then over to Haymarket to the American Express building. She was silent and he played the clown, told her jokes and anecdotes, desperate to amuse her. The more he insisted on his presence the less real it seemed to either of them.

He asked her if he could pick her up when she got off and she said she thought they might be seeing too much of each other as it was. They shook hands.

A moment after she went into the building she came out again and returned the scarf. "I can't take this from you," she said. "It's beautiful and all that but I have no right to take anything from you."

He wasn't looking at her, was looking everywhere but directly at her. "If you're going with someone, that's okay," he said. "I'm not asking for anything." He stuffed the scarf in her shoulder purse.

"I'm off at six thirty," she said in her plaintive voice.

He said he would come back for her, though when she kissed him on the mouth—her lipstick had a faint cherry taste—it left him oddly frightened.

5

When Marjorie Kirstner came into the workroom she was wearing a gray silk blouse over her topless bikini. Only a moment ago (in sensed time), he had spied her from the window sunbathing in the back garden and her sudden presence—those large pointed breasts stretching the silk—had the quality of an illusionist's trick. "Would a cold beer interest you?" she asked him. He had been lying on the couch, pages of manuscript strewn across his lap, working and sleeping, the two at once. Marjorie repeated the question, modified it. She was standing over him, legs apart, hands on hips, sucking on the fruit of her impatience.

Terman raised himself into a sitting position, felt put upon by her intrusion.

"Why are you the only one required to work?" she asked, leaving without his answer, angry at something. He stood up to meet her when she returned with two cans of Heinekens on a small tray.

"Where's your young lady friend?" she asked, giving him a beer he hadn't asked for.

"I'm not her keeper," he said.

"I'd have been most surprised if you were," she said. "She seems a very independent young person from what I can tell. I thought your young friend might like to join us in the garden."

Terman said he didn't think his young friend was on the grounds, though he could see that Marjorie was indifferent to the news, had been making idle conversation. She hung on and, wanting her gone, he invited her to take a seat.

"I have no intention of standing in the way of progress," she said. "As soon as I finish my beer, I'm returning to the garden." She looked out the window, studied the view with pointed amusement. "This room comes equipped with picture window, does it? I hope you enjoyed the view."

He pretended not to know what she meant.

She straddled a chair for a moment or two and then suggested, as if the suggestion made itself, that they take a walk around the grounds. "There's a body of water I'd like you to see."

"Is there?"

"It's a particularly lovely spot, very bucolic, very unspoiled, very relaxing."

"Is it a long walk?"

"I promise I won't tire you out," she said, "though of course I have no way of knowing what your capacities are, do I?"

He felt uneasy walking in the fields with her, suspicious and uncertain of what she wanted, wary of missing the point.

Her chatter was compulsive and he tended to listen intermittently, feeding on the odd and interesting word.

"How would you make me out in a novel?" she asked, the question addressed to herself more than to him. "You wouldn't, would you?" she answered for him. "Not bloody likely... Terman, don't you think it's smashing here?" They could see the stream now through the arch of trees.

"I never draw characters from life," he said, "unless at wit's end."

"You don't? I never heard a real writer confess that before. What you're really saying, isn't it, is that I'm not interesting enough to be in one of your precious books. Not enough one way or another, I suppose."

"Too much both ways," he said.

"Yes? What does that mean exactly? Do you think I have an undeservedly low opinion of myself. It might be, after all, that I have a low opinion of what American writers find grist for their mill."

"It could be that," he said.

She took his arm and gave it back, nothing bought ever worth the price. "I talk too much out of school. You'll forgive me if I overstated my case."

"Isn't it better to be a character of your own creation," he said, "than some shadow of yourself falsely and insufficiently imagined?"

"I'll take everything I can get, thank you," said Marjorie. "And I'll not forgive you for finding me insufficiently imaginable."

Her self-deprecation tired him and he walked along with her without further comment. She too was silent briefly, complainingly silent.

"With a view like this," Terman said, "I'm surprised you ever stay indoors."

"Max hates nature," she whispered. "He's supposed to be so visual and all that but I don't believe he ever actuallly looks outside himself."

"That's my story too," he said. "The only things I ever look at are inside my head."

"I don't believe a word of it," she said. "I think you'll say anything to make an effect if you don't mind my saying so. Are you uncomfortable being alone with me? You've been unnaturally quiet, haven't you?" She had an abrupt tentative walk as if not all the parts of her body were agreed on the same destination.

"I'm looking at the sights," he said, avoiding her eyes. "I try not to disappoint."

"The sights, is that it?" She laughed loudly, too loudly. He could feel her unacknowledged complaint rising to the surface, making ready to join them in the open air, could feel it in the edginess she generated, could feel it in the novelistic view of her his imagination allowed.

He was not a man to dissuade confidences even when he had no patience to listen to them or knew in advance, as he thought he did now, exactly what secrets awaited him.

Marjorie informed him, in a voice that belied itself with irony, of being neglected by her husband, of the lonliness and humiliation attendant on such neglect. She talked of herself as if she were the orphaned heroine of a novel of unremitting banality. Her story, though in itself heart-rending, refused sympathy and so moved him by its reticence, touched him by failing to touch him.

He kept his distance, was not about to make love to his employer's wife, a rawedged, tight-nerved woman who publicly modelled her dissatisfaction.

"It sounds as if you've been treated badly," he said.

"Like most people, I got what I bargained for, don't you think?"

The question requested denial and he said that he thought most people got worse than they deserved. He said he wondered why she had trusted him, a man she barely knew, with such personal news.

She was telling him, she said, because there was no one else to tell and he had a sympathetic face—those blue eyes—and he was a writer whose work she admired. She had once read a novel of his that spoke to her.

"What novel was it?" he asked, opening his attention to her.

It was his first, she said, withholding the title, or the first that was published in the United Kingdom. It was she, in fact, on the basis of that book, who had brought him to Max's attention and so had been midwife to what had turned into an extended collaboration.

"Then he does respect your opinion," Terman pointed out. "You can't have it both ways."

"Max used to listen to me quite a bit," she said, turning to look at something, some flash of movement, real or imagined, at the other side of the stream. "He's not the same person he was. You've seen it yourself, haven't you?"

"What I hear you saying, Marjorie, is that you think Max has got someone else." Terman had the momentary notion that his son was watching him from the deep brush on the other side of the stream. The notion was unsustaining, fled like shadows from a light.

"It's obvious, isn't it?" she was saying. "When you confront him with the news he denies everything, treats you like an escaped loony. He denies everything."

Her bitterness tortured her face. He wanted to ask her what had moved her in his book, though waited for a more appropriate time for his question. He had difficulty separating his own interests from the disinterest of listener.

"Every woman who's ever entered our house he's managed to bed down one way or another," she said.

"You're exaggerating, I think."

"Everyone," she insisted, aware of the implication for Terman, a mad thin smile invading her stoic's mouth. "I have evidence," she added mysteriously. "What do you think Sylvie and I were talking about when you watched us from the window?"

Her assertion evoked a passionate denial. "Marjorie, why should I watch you from the window?"

She laughed, a temporary distraction from abiding discontent. "I was joking," she said. "Didn't you look even a little? I was hoping you'd look."

He said he regretted the missed opportunity, feeling the regret as he announced it. It was odd how language sometimes created a reality in its wake.

"I forced a confession out of Sylvie," Marjorie said. "She denied it at first absolutely and categorically and I simply said, Sylvie you don't have to lie to me, I'm fully aware of what's going on. She kept to her story until she saw that I wasn't buying a word of it, then she admitted that she'd been sleeping with my husband on and off for three years. I was horrified. You're a friend of mine, I said to her, how could you possibly do something like that? Max wouldn't let me alone, she said. Then she cried and asked me to forgive her."

They came to a stile. "This is where our property ends," she said.

"How do you know there were others?" Terman asked.

"You'll find out about it soon enough," she said. "When Max wants something—I know this from having lived with him for fourteen years—he'll stop at literally nothing to get what he wants."

Her discontent seemed contagious.

"He can't help himself," she said in his defense. "He's addicted to having absolutely everything he wants."

"If what you say is true, why do you stay with him?" It struck him, listening to himself, that his question couldn't have been more predictable and banal had she written his lines for him.

"I really don't see how I can continue living with him," she said in a world-weary voice. "Yet of course one goes on, one must."

"We ought to be getting back," he said. (He didn't say that; it was what, not quite listening to the next stage of her confidence, he had wanted to say.) It was before or after she had turned her ankle by stepping on a rock or distended root and found herself unable to walk. She sat on the grass forlornly, alternatly squeezing and stroking the injured ankle to assuage the pain. Terman offered his hand, suggested she walk lightly on the ankle rather that let it stiffen up.

"Don't you see," she said with sudden vehemence, "that this film your working on will never get made."

He was leaning over her, offering his hand, a crazed sky overhead. "I don't believe you," he said, though it was not disbelief he was talking about, not that so much as his disinclination to share her pain.

"It's gone on too long," she said. "You know what I'm talking about."

When he withdrew his hand, she asked if he was planning to leave her there.

"Why don't you try to get up?"

"Why don't you go and get some help? I'm not going to be able to walk."

"You want me to go or you don't?"

"I'm putting myself in your hands," she said.

Terman squatted next to her, the posture precarious. "Let me look at the ankle," he said. It was swollen slightly and would swell more. He didn't know what he was looking for, what significances, and was aggrieved at the ankle for being in complicity with its owner. "You can lean your weight on me," he said. "We can get back to the house that way." It was beginning to rain delicately.

"I think I'm too big for you," she said. "Do you know how much I weigh?"

"It's a matter of public record," he said.

Marjorie, who was almost his height, got to her feet with his help, balancing herself on her good ankle. For some reason they found themselves in an embrace.

She moaned twice for each step they took, asked again and again if she were too heavy for him until the weight of the question were almost as heavy a burden as the woman herself. He was surprised at how leaden she felt, at the deadness of her weight.

The rain was a fine mist, a veil of grief. Walking with her in the drizzle, holding her up, her arm clamped around his neck, he sensed that someone was watching them through the sights of a gun.

Just on the other side of the stile, at the place where the pond reentered view, he lost his balance. She dug her nails into his chest as they fell.

She apologized for her weight.

"It wasn't your fault," he said. "The grass was slick and my feet gave out."

"You're not attracted to me," she said, "are you?" She disentangled herself, her teeth clenched against impending pain. "There's no pleasure in our contact, is there?"

In pain himself, Terman had difficulty focusing on Marjorie's complaint. "You're an attractive woman, Marjorie," he said.

"That ought to hold the old bitch a while," she said. "Who the hell do you think you are?" She squeezed the neck of her ankle, punished and encouraged it.

His hip hurt but he was able to stand up without difficulty. He stretched the muscles of his legs, first the right then the left, then the right again. When he stretched the right leg, and only at a certain point, he could feel the stinging pains in his hip.

"Well," she said, "what now?"

He studied the landscape to see if there was anyone in the near distance he might hail; the area was oddly desolate.

"It'll have to be on the left side this time," he said, holding out his hand.

"Have you hurt yourself?" she asked. "I can't say how sorry I am."

He saw no point in denying it—he had long since stopped perceiving himself as a hero—though he was embarrassed at the extent of her apparent concern, the exaggeration of real feeling.

"Sit down and rest a few minutes," she said, sliding back a few feet so that the leaves of a large oak screened some of the rain.

"We ought to get some care for that ankle," he said.

"If I don't mind, why should you? It's very beautiful here, isn't it, very still and very beautiful.

The view, what he could see of it from where they sat, did not strike him as beautiful. It merely satisfied expectation. Nature, it was true, never seemed to him as beautiful or surprising as art. One had the difficulty of course of only being able to see patches of it at one time, fragments of some presumably larger design. He mentioned this heresy to her and got a blank look in return, an almost shocked stare. He resisted apology.

When they got back to the cottage Max and the others still hadn't returned. There was a message for an L. Turpin on the desk in the workroom that someone had called, though the name of the caller was not given (the note was barely legible), nor was there a return number. He asked Sylvie, who was in the living room reading a copy of *Vogue,* if she had taken the phone call for him. Her manner was vague though earnest. She could tell from studying the handwriting that the note to him was not her work. Not only hadn't she answered the phone, she said, she had no recollection of having heard it ring. Who else was in the house? he asked.

#

Marjorie sat in the workroom with her injured leg propped up on a stool, holding an unlit cigar in her long fingers as a prop.

Terman was trying to figure out Tom's next move and thought it possible, or not impossible, that his son was somewhere on the grounds of the Kirstner estate.

"You *are* distracted, aren't you?" she said. "Tuppence for them."

He said he was thinking of food and Marjorie said she thought there was some fruit in a cut glass bowl in the dining room, granny smiths, bananas, and dark grapes.

Terman went into the dining room and returned empty-handed, something else impelling him, something he couldn't remember or had never quite known.

"Wasn't my fruit any good?" she asked.

He glanced at his watch. It was ten minutes to seven—another day irretrievably gone. "When are they coming back?" he asked, the question rhetorical.

She shook her head in a self-amused way, smiling charmingly at him. "I wonder if you could get me an aperitif," she said.

Fixed on something else, he only partly heard her request, wary of her demands, thinking that no matter the language she was asking him to make love to her.

"I'd like something to warm me up," she said.

They could hear Sylvie upstairs talking on the phone in French, complaining about something.

Marjorie put her finger over her lips, enjoining him to silence. When Sylvie's conversation was completed, Marjorie said, "You are forgetful, you know. I'm worried about you."

Sylvie came downstairs, stuck her head in the room then disappeared somewhere outside.

Terman poured a glass of Rafael for Marjorie and made himself a Scotch, not bothering to put in ice or water, wanting to feel the heat of the liquor in his chest. He tossed down the drink and poured himself a second, before delivering the aperitif to Marjorie.

She acknowledged his service with a wink. "Would you change the compress on my ankle, my friend?" she asked in her peremptory way. "You don't really mind, do you?"

He was unwrapping the compress when he heard a car pull into the driveway and he momentarily observed himself, bent devotedly over her outstretched leg, from the viewpoint of someone coming in them. "The swelling is down," he said. "It can't be too serious."

"My dear, everything is too serious," she said with a wink. "It's such a bore, isn't it?" It was as if an understanding had been established between them, an unacknowledged intimacy.

After dinner Terman sought out Isabelle who was sitting some distance from him at the large table. "I'm going back to London," he whispered. "There's no more for me to do here."

"I understand," she said coldly.

"Would you like to go?"

"Are you asking me to come with you?"

He noticed that Marjorie, leaning on a cane by the kitchen door, was watching them.

"That's what I'm asking," he said. "I don't understand what else you thought."

"Are we having a fight?" she asked.

"Let's go into another room and talk."

"I don't want to," she said, brushing off his arm.

He walked away, then came back to her. "It would please me if you came along," he said.

She followed him outside to the car, neither consenting nor refusing, smiling apologetically to whomever she passed. Marjorie was watching them from the kitchen.

"You look very sexy tonight," he said. He was holding the passenger door open for her (or for anyone) when he had an intuition that someone was observing them from the woods just beyond the garden.

"I'll go with you," she said, "but I have to get my things first and say goodbye to the others, which will take a few minutes. Is that all right? I know how impatient you get, but it's not my nature to accept people's hospitality without thanking them."

He sat in the car and watched her walk back toward the house, full of frail determination, glancing over her shoulder to make sure that he hadn't gone off without her.

Max came out after several minutes, followed by Isabelle who turned around to say something in the doorway to someone else. He heard Marjorie's authoritative voice, heard his name mentioned.

"Wish we could have had more time together," Max was saying, his face at the window like a Halloween mask, "but as I've told you more than you want to hear I'm not my own man." He let himself into the back seat of the car, lowered his voice to the sympathetic tone he used for playing the good guy, the one who if not pressured by forces outside his control would give Terman everything he wanted. Terman, seeking comfort, let himself be gulled. It was not what Max said that was so persuasive but the undiguised need to persuade that worked its charm.

"The women are watching us," Max said. "Regard."

Indeed, Marjorie and Isabelle—Marjorie leaning on her cane—were standing silently just inside the doorway, looking out at the car. "What did Marjorie say to you about me?" he asked.

"I don't think your name ever came up," Terman said.

"You did spend some time with her, did you? And she had nothing, either good or bad, to say about yours truly?"

The two women, Marjorie's hand at the small of Isabelle's back, approached them.

"A bit frightening, the two of them in tandem, don't you think?"

Isabelle looked into the back seat where Max was sitting and said hello.

"We're talking shop," Max said.

"Are you?" said Marjorie, offering them a road show version of her unconvincingly merciless grande dame. "I had the impression that Terman and Isabelle were going to London and we had come to the car to say goodbye to them."

"I'm sitting in the car," Max said, "so if Terman and Isabelle drive off they'll have to take me along as bloody hostage."

"He doesn't get drunk like other people," Marjorie explained to

Isabelle, "he merely behaves oddly."

"Is it odd, I ask you, to have a conference with my conspirator? We'll put the question to Isabelle whose biases are either unknown or non-existent."

"When Terman makes up his mind to go somewhere, he wants to be at that place in the flash of an eye," Isabelle said. "That's the way he is, I'm afraid."

"Are you in a hurry, son?" Max asked. "Is there time for a word or two between us?"

"It's cold as a witch's tit," Marjorie said. "I'm going back to the cottage if no one minds." She blew them a kiss then turned to go, though didn't.

"I'll help you back," Isabelle said, taking her arm.

Marjorie pulled away, said she preferred making it on her own if that didn't interfere with anyone else's plans. She took four maybe five steps and fell heavily. Neither of the men got out of the car. Isabelle hurried to her and asked Marjorie, who was making an effort not to cry, if she hurt herself. "I feel like letting out an enormous scream," Marjorie said.

"One of us ought to go out there," Max said. "It would be a great favor to me, Terman, if you represented the partnership on this occasion. Just tell her that Max sent you, that you've come in place of Max."

Marjorie was on her feet, moving unsteadily toward the house, Isabelle followed protectively a step behind. "No need," Marjorie said over her shoulder.

Terman opened his window to call to either or both of the women, but could think of nothing he wanted to say.

He looked into the rearview mirror and noted that Max was slumped like a ragdoll against the back of the seat. "Are you all right, Max?" he asked. There was no answer for the longest time. "Max!"

The eyes opened with apparent reluctance, or offered that illusion in the dark. The voice boomed in the closed space. "Why don't you wait until the morning, old son?" it said. "Nothing useful or enobling can be done at this time of blight. Am I not speaking truth?" He let himself out of the car, opened his fly and peed in a wide arc toward the house. "Serve them right if they get a whiff of that."

Terman could hardly make out the numbers on his watch, studying its unillumined face in the dark car, refusing to turn on the light or open the door. He squalled Isabelle's name through the partially opened window and thought he heard it echo back after a time lapse of several seconds. It was possible that he heard Tom crawling through the brush like a commando, gradually approaching the car, stopping every few minutes to disguise his progress. The gun was in his hand as he crawled, held just above the ground so as not to get fouled by dirt or twigs. In two more sequences, he would be close enough to open fire at the silhouette in the driver's seat.

The assassin in the woods rested for a count of five—Terman counting the seconds to himself as he imagined the other doing—then crawled the final thirty feet to the garden's edge.

A few seconds later, he heard footsteps and he threw himself across the seat, hands over his head, to avoid the gunshots he anticipated. There were a series of raps like machine gun fire at some great distance. Isabelle's face was at the opposing window, slightly distorted by his perspective.

"You don't mean to sleep in the car, darling, do you?" she was saying. She opened the door on the passenger side to make herself understood.

He lifted his head to give her space to sit down, unable to give up the idea that an assassin awaited him just outside the window of the car. When she was seated and had closed the door he put his head in her lap.

"If we're not going to London," she said, "we ought to go inside, don't you think?"

He could smell her sea-scent beneath the wool of her pants—the wool rough agaist his face—mingling with her perfume and something else, something not quite defineable. The pants had a fly and he worked the zipper open with his teeth.

She slapped at the back of his head, half reprimand, half play. "Mind," she said.

Her smell had depths like a well-aged wine, though seemed somewhat murky as if it hadn't travelled well or had been shaken up in transport. She wore a bikini under the mannish pants, an odd conjunction, an aspect (he thought) of disguise.

Terman had not thought of Isabelle as overpoweringly sexy before, was never so taken with her as this moment in the car with his head like some rooting animal buried in her crotch.

Isabelle offered no encouragement, even held the back of his neck with her hand as if (though not seriously) to restrain him from going further. He found an arm cramped under him and he used it, despite the stiffness in his shoulder, the numbness of the tips of his fingers, to open her pants at the waist. She murmured something, neither assent nor complaint, some English cry or sigh he had never understood. He thought of it, if he thought of anything, as getting to the bottom of Isabelle.

Intoxicated by her scent, his nose, that surrogate pointer, forced its way between her legs. The scent had not even its usual pleasure for him—something murky and contravening in it—yet he pursued it with some urgency, tracked it to its source.

The taste was different too this time—she opened for him to taste, her first compliance in the cramped silence—like a great wine twenty years past its peak, not quite gone bad though beginning to turn.

At any moment a gunshot might come through the window and tear off the top of his head. He thought of that, or the thought touched the edge of consciousness, as he supped at her well. For that space of awareness, he sucked on terror, dying and reviving, frightened to death.

She wanted him on top of her, she whispered, and he was aware at least for that moment that she was there too.

He was, oddly, in no special hurry and she had to tug on his arm to bring him to her, to remind him of her request. And that too, the fucking itself, was as good as he could remember it. He said or meant to say it, his mouth at her ear, hearing gunshots in his dreams as he slept, his weight centered on her.

The bullet took a devious path, wound itself around his head before going in one ear and coming out the other.

#

It was almost four AM when she woke him, the time in his head corresponding to the clock in the car. She was buttoning his shirt, though that may only have been the last part of it, his pants already restored, fly closed, belt buckled.

When he was finally awake—who could say how long it took?—he felt lightened and refreshed. He started up the car without a word to Isabelle, without even the barest acknowledgement. She curled up in her seat and he covered her with his jacket, his tenderness lasting only for the duration of the gesture. He had woken angry, its object undefined.

The night yielded by degrees. He was more than halfway to London when the cause of his anger clarified, the message deciphering itself as he drove. Isabelle had slept with Max, said intuition, and intuition almost never deceived him. He felt disappointment, not much more than that, grieved privately at the insufficiency of his passion. *I ought to break Max in half,* he thought. And if not Max, who?

Isabelle was asleep when he arrived at the Holland Park house and he left her as she was—a light coming from the second floor study he wanted to investigate—to go inside. "Don't leave me," she called after him as he returned to the car in delayed response.

In sleep, she appeared childlike and fragile, an innocent, unprotected by the disguises of will.

He had difficulty waking her. When he whispered her name a shadow of pain scarred her face. Her eyes opened and closed like a doll's eyes.

"What do you want?" she asked, mildly indignant.

"Do you want me to carry you in?" he asked.

"I should say not," she said, sitting up stiffly, moving her hair out of her eyes. "I don't know what's the matter with me. I never fall asleep in cars."

Isabelle hurried ahead of him into the house.

She would have said something to him, had something on her mind, but thought to go upstairs first to take a bath.

The delay frustrated him. He wanted the ritual of her confession (and his forgiveness) out of the way so that they could get on to something else.

They had barely exchanged a word since he had wakened her, the silence echoing. The unspoken secret rankled.

Terman was conscious of what he did only in the moment of its doing, taunted afterward by the consequences of unremembered actions. The cry of the kettle disconcerted him—he had no sense of having gone into the kitchen to put up water for tea—thought in his distraction that there was a child in the house or an aggrieved cat.

"Tea or coffee?" he called up the stairs. He knew the answer, but he wanted to hear the sound of a voice, something to confirm his presence in the world.

On the way upstairs, he forgot about the boiled water in the kitchen, the question of tea or coffee, the sound of Isabelle's voice or anyone else's, and directed himself to his study, the only room he felt at home in. It was not as if he didn't know what he would find or not find when he pulled open the bottom drawer of the desk. It was merely that he had to see for himself again and again, had to hold illusion only to court disillusion. A quixotic belief in the infinite possibilities of restoration compelled him. Surprises were never a surprise. He found a toy pistol in the very place he had kept the real one, a mock redemption, a menacing joke. He studied the imitation disbelievingly, half-thought that the original gun had been false too—everything on close inspection was false—though he knew that wasn't the case. It was at that moment he decided that he could not be at ease with himself until Tom returned home.

#

Close up of a railway timetable. A hand circles 2:07 with a fountain pen. Wipe to a railway clock at two minutes after two. A slow pan reveals a railway station somewhere in Eastern Europe. There are four people waiting without apparent urgency for the train, an old couple, a middleaged woman who looks like a madam, and a studious-looking young man carrying a briefcase.

We see the hand of the clock move to 2:08. We hear a train coming into the station, hear it before we see it. The train slows down as it approaches the station but then as it appears about to stop, picks up speed again. The old man knocks at the side with his walking stick, calling to it to stop. "What's the meaning of this?" he says to the others. "I demand to know the meaning of this." "Shhh," his wife says. The train flashes by leaving a cloud of dust in the air. When the train is gone, we are made aware of a shadowy form on the tracks. The stationmaster comes out after a moment to have a look. In the wake of the train, we discover the body of a young woman lying on the tracks. The four people on the platform pretend not to see what surely each has glimpsed at some point.

We cut away to the dashboard clock of Henry Berger's car. It reads 2:04, then 2:05. Henry Berger and Yanna are travelling at high speed along a winding road. A black limousine seems to be following them, though perhaps it is only going in the same direction.

"Are we almost there?" the woman asks with a kind of private irony.

"We are always almost there," says Berger. "There's the station up ahead, an idyllic setting isn't it? Don't get out of the car until I tell you it's all right."

We cut to two stationworkers lifting the body, covered with a blanket, off the tracks. The stationmaster stands behind them waving a red flag. The railway station clock reads 2:07.

We see Berger through the window of the station talking to the stationmaster. The studious young man, looking in the window, appears to be interested in their conversation.

We see the limousine that had been behind them on the road pull into the station lot in the row just behind Berger's car. Yanna rolls up the window, locks the door, watches the other car in her rear-view mirror. The oddly dressed woman from the station gets into the other car.

Berger returns to the parking lot on the run, gets into his car. "We have to go to the next station," he says. "The train was five minutes early and didn't stop."

From an overview we see three cars in close proximity—Berger's in the lead—speeding along a narrow road. The red sportscar shoots past Berger in a dangerous maneuver. As soon as it gets ahead, it slows up, forcing Berger and the black limousine behind him to decrease their pace.

The limousine moves out alongside Berger's car and we see into it for the first time. There are two heavyset men in front, both wearing dark glasses, and the heavily made-up woman from the station in the back. When the young woman removes her wig—we catch a glimpse of her as the limousine goes by—her appearance is significantly altered. The two cars speed ahead of Berger, concerned for the moment only with each other. At some point the second car moves abreast of the first, neither making an effort to pass or fall back. We perceive them from Berger's vantage point, losing them momentarily each time the road turns. Yanna hunkers down in her seat, covers her eyes with her hands. The two cars bump one another, each trying to force the other off the road. At some point the driver of the sports car throws something through the window at the other car. There is an explosion, the limousine crashing into a telephone poll. The sports car speeds on. A man in woman's clothing, his clothes in flames, pulls himself out of the wrecked car. He staggers a few moments, then collapses. Berger and Yanna stop a few yards behind the wreck, get out of their car. The transvestite dies before they can get to him/her. (We recognize the figure as Pietro D'Agostino.) They return to their car and sit at the side of the road, Berger's arm around Yanna, who is shivering. She kisses him.

Yanna: When I'm frightened I always want to make love.

Berger starts up the car and they move on. Through the rear-view mirror we see the scattered fragments of the wreck, streams of flame illuminating the countryside.

#

Terman returned to the kitchen and made two cups of Indian tea, using one tea bag for both cups, an uncharacterisic economy. He drank half a cup diluted with milk and poured the rest down the drain. Isabelle's would be cold when she finished whatever she was doing and he called to her in a tentative voice, tea's ready, not insisting on it, wanting above all to avoid a fight.

When she came down in jeans and a cashmere sweater, her hair in curlers covered by a red scarf, he asked her if she wanted to go back to sleep. She said, thank you no. A formality had come between them, a delicate caution.

One word, he felt, a wrong word or one readily misconstrued, might precipitate a fight. He was determined to prevent conflict if possible and was all smiles and kindness for a moment or two. "You're not acting like yourself," she told him.

Something else was on his mind and though he had resolved not to mention it to Isabelle, obsession overrode constraint.

"I'm thinking of sending Tom back to the states," he announced.

She got up to make herself a fresh pot of tea. "Are you?" she asked.

He would be able to breathe again, he said, once his son was off his chest. Isabelle said nothing. He repeated his remark.

"You've got twenty-four hours to get out of town, pardner," she said, her eyes mysteriously wet.

"You do that very well," he said.

Isabelle wore her impatient look. "You can't make him leave if he doesn't want to go, Terman, can you?"

He put his hand on her hand, reaching awkwardly across the table. "He'll go, I think."

"Why should he, for God's sake. Why the hell should he? If you were in his place, would you go?" She suffered his touch, her will clenched against him.

He withdrew his hand, said he didn't understand her bitterness, that it was Tom he was talking about, not her.

"Oh cut it out," she screamed at him.

Afterward, when they had agreed on the terms of a truce and Isabelle had gone up to their room for no clear reason, a dull pain moved into his chest, frightening him. He staggered up from the table, dislodging the cup of cold tea in front of him, and fled into the nearer of the two sitting rooms, a hand on his chest pressing back the invisible ache. He willed calm, sat with his eyes closed, setting up the itinerary of mundane tasks that would occupy him for the next three or four hours. Hot bath...brush teeth...shave...shop at Europa for beer... read last two chapters of *Dom Casmura*...take Isabelle to lunch....

The pain receded or moved on, exorcised by the litany of his plans and he went upstairs to put up water for his bath. He was taking off his shirt when he heard a crash from somewhere in the house. He stuck his head out the door and called Isabelle's name and got nothing but a squeak of wind against window in return. When he looked into the bedroom she raised her head and asked if something was the matter. "Do you want to make love?" he asked, not knowing what else to say. "When I wake up," she said and he returned to the bathroom and closed himself in. The ache in his chest recalled itself like an echo.

Terman looked crumpled in the mirror, more so without his clothes than with, catching his reflection out of the side of his eye as he stepped into the tub.

The water in the bath was too hot on the surface and not warm enough once he was seated in it, an underlay of coldish water like a draft at the bottom. Had he locked the door? It worried him that he hadn't, made aware of the vulnerabilty of his position. He stood up and sat down again, would take the risk.

The idea of a bath was to give oneself to it unequivocally, to ripen in the hot water like noodles or potatoes. It had to be searing for that, almost too hot to bear. He slid forward so that only his head and the top of his knees weren't submerged. He was thinking of the best way of breaking the news to Tom, rehearsing variant possibilities in his imagination, nothing right. *Tom, I want you to go home: I'm sending you home.* His anger trampled his prose. *You come all the way from America to visit and then you don't even live with me, though invade my life, steal from my desk, leave threatening messages. I won't stand for it any longer.* Empty bluster. He had begun to sound like his own father. Perhaps he ought to take some of the responsibility on himself. *I can't even handle my own life, how can I handle yours?*

Someone was knocking on the door to the bathroom. "I'm in the bath," he said. After a moment, assuming she hadn't heard him, he raised his voice, said he hadn't fallen asleep in the tub. She made no comment or none that he could hear. "I'll be out in a few minutes," he said.

He felt no compelling urgency to leave the bath but it was time and he emerged dutifully, moving quickly to circumvent the shock of air, throwing a bath towel over his shoulders.

He shaved and dressed, held brief consultation with his reflection in the steamy mirror ("I worry that you'll do something desparate," he said to his son) and came down the stairs like a visiting dignitary. Isabelle was asleep on the couch, dead asleep as she had been in the car, a french fashion magazine called *Marie Clare* clutched to her chin. Terman tried to remove the magazine without disturbing her sleep, but she held on with the ferocity of a child. He went away, then came back with his trench coat from the closet and covered her legs. After kissing the top of her head, he tried again to remove the magazine but Isabelle held fast.

There was a week's mail, mostly bills and circulars (what else was there ever?) stacked neatly in two piles on the dining room table. Leafing through, he remembered he had a letter from Magda in his jacket pocket that he had been carrying around for two days. It had been posted nine days ago from New York so was likely to be old news. His right hand trembling like something in a wind, he tore the letter open, wanting to get the distasteful out of the way so he could get on to something else.

Typed on thin yellow paper, the letter was written in capitals like a ransom note.

LUKAS...EXCUSE THE BROKEN TYPEWRITER. IT'S ALL I HAVE AT THE MOMENT. SINCE YOUR TELEGRAM ARRIVED I HAVEN'T BEEN ABLE TO SLEEP THINKING ABOUT TOM. I WOULD HAVE PHONED BUT AS YOU KNOW YOUR NUMBER ISN'T LISTED AND YOU NEVER SAW FIT TO TRUST IT TO ME. MY FIRST IMPULSE WAS TO GET A FLIGHT AND COME OVER IMMEDIATELY, THOUGH IT WOULD MEAN TAKING OFF FROM MY JOB. THEN I THOUGHT NO, TOM'S IN YOUR CUSTODY FOR THE SUMMER AND YOU HAVE FULL RESPONSIBILITY. WHY SHOULD IT BE EASIER FOR HIS MOTHER TO HANDLE HIM THAN HIS FATHER? LET ME GET TO THE POINT OF THIS COMMUNICATION. TOM IS QUITE ERRATIC. OTHER PEOPLE HAVE TOLD ME THIS SO YOU DON'T HAVE TO RELY ON MY PERCEPTION ALONE. HE CAN BE VERY REASONABLE ONE MOMENT, VERY CHARMING, THEN GO OFF AND DO SOMETHING DISCOMBOBULATING THE NEXT. I'VE TRIED TO GET HIM TO SEE A THERAPIST BUT HE ABSOLUTELY REFUSES TO GO. A FATHER'S INFLUENCE IN THAT DIRECTION MIGHT HAVE MADE SOME DIFFERENCE. THE POINT I'M MAKING IS THAT HE'S A STRANGE BOY AND UNLIKELY TO BECOME LESS STRANGE WITHOUT OUTSIDE HELP. HIS FREINDS, I'M AFRAID, TEND TO BE BAD INFLUENCES IN ALL THE OBVIOUS WAYS. I DON'T THINK YOU WOULD LIKE THEM ANY MORE THAN I DO, I REALLY DON'T. THEY'RE MOSTLY COLLEGE DROPOUTS WITHOUT REGULAR JOBS AND LEAD WHAT MIGHT BE DESCRIBED AS MARGINAL EXISTENCES. SOME DRUGS INVOLVED, I SHOULD IMAGINE. I'VE BEEN GOING AROUND IN CIRCLES NOT SAYING EXACTLY WHAT I MEAN. FRIENDS OF MINE HAVE INVITED ME TO STAY WITH THEM IN NEW HAMPSHIRE DURING MY VACATION IN AUGUST, A VACATION LONG OVERDUE AND DESPERATELY AWAITED. I'D LIKE TO KNOW THAT TOM IS ALL RIGHT BEFORE I TAKE OFF AND THAT YOU'LL KEEP HIM WITH YOU UNTIL I RETURN ON SEPTEMBER 3. I HOPE YOU CAN PUT HIM IN CONTACT WITH SOME SYMPATHETIC PEOPLE HIS OWN AGE. THE COMBI-

NATION OF BAD COMPANIONS AND NOT HAVING A FATHER IN THE HOUSE HAVE HAD A DELETERIOUS EFFECT ON TOM. THIS MAY BE AN OPPORTUNITY FOR YOU TO UNDO SOME OF THE DAMAGE. I'D APPRECIATE A PHONE CALL AT YOUR EARLIEST CONVENIENCE TO LET ME KNOW HOW HE'S DOING.

M.

Terman went up to his study, put an air letter in his Lettera 32 and typed off an answer in white heat, resisting the impulse to do the text in lower case.

Dear Magda,

I am writing to acknowledge your letter which didn't reach me until...

Terman addressed the airletter, assembled it and put it in the inside pocket of his jacket. He thought if he viewed his own behavior from the vantage of an outsider, he might well despise himself. His watch, which was going again, indicated that it was almost 9 o'clock, that the real day had begun.

He unlocked the door of his hermetic space and stepped out into the hall, wary of the least shadow. The house was quiet, unnaturally silent. He restrained an impulse to shout, walked stealthily, lit his way in the muted morning light from room to room.

Isabelle was asleep in the master bedroom, had changed location (had sleep-walked?) while he was writing the letter to Magda. The other rooms, including both bathrooms, were empty.

He mounted the stairs to the third floor with the same stealth, though the creaky stair boards contrived to betray his step.

Even before he reached the top of the steps he called his son's name. He heard his own name in response but it came from below.

"Terman?"

In a moment there were footsteps on the stairs coming up, a delayed echo.

"What time is it?" Isabelle asked him. "I feel as if I've been out of it for hours."

He opened each of the five rooms on the third floor, pushing the doors open with his foot and stepping back. He tried the closets (once started it was difficult to give up the quest), looked under the beds, uncovered nothing. "Could I talk to you, Terman?" Isabelle asked.

In one of the rooms, the one with the full length wall mirrors, there was a chair by the window overlooking the street that he could have sworn had not been in that position before. It was the only obvious sign that someone might have been there.

"In my dream," Isabelle was saying, "you were having a fight with my mother and I was trying to meliorate. You kept insisting—we both thought you were bonkers—that though you were younger than she, you were actually her father."

"I was speaking metaphorically," Terman said.

"My mother kept repeating—it was something she used to say to me when I was a child—"You make me want to tear my hair, luv."

When they were downstairs he asked Isabelle if she had knocked on the bathroom door when he was in the bath.

"Why would I do that?"

"You didn't, did you?"

"Of course I didn't." She lit a filter-tipped cigar, stared unhappily into the smoke.

He prowled the house, opening and reopening the same doors. Since when had she been smoking cigars, he wondered.

"Once you start something," she said, "you never give it up, do you?" She put an arm around his waist, though removed it almost immediately.

"Don't you give me a hard time too," he said.

"Who's giving whom a hard time, I'd like to know."

If Tom were gone, he thought, everything else would fall into place. Isabelle left him to make a phone call from the kitchen with the door closed.

He shouted Tom's name so that it reverberated through the seemingly untenanted house.

Isabelle returned as if he had conjured her from out of the walls. "If I were your son," she said, "I'd probably hide from you too." She winked at him to soften the remark.

He was in no mood to be propitiated, was up to the worst she had to offer. "If I were me, I'd hide from me too," he said. "You don't think he's still in the house, do you?"

"I don't see how he could be," she said, "do you?"

At first he couldn't find his corduroy jacket, and was willing to blame his son for that loss too, but then it turned up on the back of a chair in the kitchen. "I'm going out to find Tom," he said. "We can go out for lunch at a wine pub when I get back if you like."

Isabelle shrugged. "I find this all so unpleasant and painful, do you know? I tend to identify with Tom and wish to God you just let us be . . . I'm sorry, sweetheart." She came over and leaned her head on his cheek. "Why don't you at least call first and see if he's there?" She kissed his face.

"Don't comfort me," he said.

"That wasn't what I had in mind," she said. "Would you like to have a go?" She winked at him in parody of brazenness.

It disturbed him when she wasn't herself, made him feel he didn't know her, that the person he knew no longer existed. He wanted to tell her that he loved her, but found the words embarrassing to speak. "I can't concentrate on anything," he said.

"I've never known you to turn it down before."

"Think of it as a postponement," he said. "One can't always do what one wants to do."

"I know all too well how that is," she said, holding the outside door open for him. "Sorry I asked."

He almost expected the boy to spring out at him as he stepped into the air.

"I have to go to work at two," she called after him. "I forgot to tell you."

#

And then the oddest thing happened. Driving in the general area of his son's rented room, he couldn't find the street, was failed by his usually faultless sense of direction. He could neither find the right street nor remember its name. It was not even that the neighborhood was foreign to him, not that excuse, nor that there were no recognizable landmarks. He came on a rather grim playground he had once played tennis in and a church in the process of being torn down that he had passed on foot a number of times, but his son's street, which ran parallel or perpendicular to it, eluded him. If only he could recall its unappealing name, he could stop someone and ask directions. Chepstow kept coming to mind, though that was the name of the proprietress, the street something else. He knew the number was 44, which was his age on his birthday before last. After a point, on something called Barlby—it was as if a syllable had been swallowed—he pulled over to the curb and stopped the car. He poked into the glove compartment to check out the ratty London street guide he kept there, though, like his memory, that too was gone.

He emptied his pockets, found a number of fragmentary messages on torn-off pieces of envelope, much of it at this point in unbreakable code. Tom's address was not among the debris.

With no clear intent he got out of the car, thought on foot he might find his son's rooming house or some familiar street name that would lead him to it. Perhaps he thought nothing of the kind, wanting merely to be out of the car, to be free of that burden.

The streets seemed to wind back on each other, but he walked energetically in a direction he had chosen arbitrarily, guided if at all by a trust in instinct. The buildings he passed were in states of disrepair, many uninhabited, some boarded up. He persisted in the sense that he was going in the right direction, took long strides—the faster he walked the less his bruised hip bothered him—anticipating that the next street (or the one after that) would be the one he sought. Never for a moment did he consider that he might be lost, or that a house with a Bed and Breakfast sign in the window might not after a certain point appear before him. It was one of those London days in which, though it appears not to be raining, almost everything is moist—the rain seeming to come up from the ground rather than down from the sky. He had the illusion from time to time that there were footseps behind him, but instead of looking to see who it was he quickened his pace.

Three Arabs standing in front of a pub, stared at him as he passed. One called something to him in a nearly incomprehensible dialect. The others laughed unpleasantly.

Did he know the man who spoke to him? He didn't think so, though turned, despite his sense of urgency, to look. Something, a stone perhaps, hit him just above the right eye. He let out a scream, the sound like nothing he had heard himself utter before, his hand to his eye. The Arabs scattered, each taking a separate direction. The scream continued, despite his intent to stop, sustained itself like an electronic alarm that had to run its course. An older man, also dark-skinned (Indian or Pakistani, he thought) came over and said something unintelligble, the persisting scream overriding other voices.

His hand came away from his eye, unglued itself from the wound. He had not, as feared, lost sight in the eye, though his vision, perhaps from the pressure of his hand, was somewhat blurred. There was a little blood from the wound, not much, insufficient to his response, the palm of his hand the wound's mirror.

Terman had embarrassed himself enough for one morning, refused the offer of the man's arm, thanked him as an afterthought, and hurried off in the direction he had come.

The man followed briefly, offering a hospital or something that sounded like hospital as if he had one in his possession. He said repeatedly that he was okay, that no real damage had been done.

And then, he had difficulty retracing his steps, the street names not what they were. The walk back seemed to age him. After a half dozen blocks, he was too tired to go any further and he sat down on a bench in front of an abandoned church, took out a handkerchief and wiped the rain from his face. In a moment or so he would get up and locate a public telephone (that consideration sustaining him), and report to Isabelle his painful misadventure. Sweetheart, she would say, I'm so sorry.

Her pity, in his imagination of it, was more than he could bear. Why, if she were as devoted to him as she pretended, had she gone off with Max?

Oh Terman, she would say—or was it Luke?—you are a misery, luv, aren't you?

He continued to sit, clasping himself against the damp air. People passed occasionally, glancing at him with indifference. He imagined himself getting up, locating a Newsagent on the next street or the next, buying a *Guardian* to get some change—mostly he avoided the English papers—locating a phone box, closing himself in, dialing his number. All he really had to do was get back to his car on Barlby Street and drive himself home.

When he looked up he saw the Pakistani and another swarthy man coming down the street toward him. Their impending presence moved him to cross the street, his gesture making it clear, he hoped, that he didn't want to be interfered with again. The Pakistani called something to him and he shouted back, "Nothing to worry about, thank you."

What the hell did they want with him? He turned right at the next corner, though he couldn't remember if he had come that way or not. It was the shock of it that caused him to lose his poise. On the next corner, standing with his back to him, was the Arab that had thrown the stone at him. (Had he thrown the stone because he recognized Terman as a Jew?) Stupidly—he knew it was a mistake to call attention to himself even as he gave vent to the impulse—he broke into a run. Not looking back, he took a left turn at the next corner, a narrow winding street called Vashti Lane, which connected with a series of other winding streets. His sense of direction betrayed him. He hurried from one tortuous street to the next only to discover himself returned to the very street from which he had taken precipitous leave.

He stood awhile against the wall at the intersection of Calgary Road and Vashti Lane before daring to look around the corner. His adversaries were standing across the street in front of a red and white stucco house, their backs to him, heads close together like conspirators. It was at moments like this that he was most aware of being in a foreign country, of having nowhere in particular to turn in a crisis. Panic governed him. He returned up the series of winding streets, running at first, then walking quickly, atempting a new set of choices. Whatever he did, his choices blind, he found himself back on Calgary Road, his original point of departure. A third time (or was it the fourth?) he reversed himself, varying his route, taking two successive lefts then a right then another half right and another, until he found himself in a *cul de sac,* a medium-high fence backing on a small unkempt field. In all of the maze of streets he had come, there had not been one open shop or a single working public telephone.

There was no entrance to the field at his end. Nothing to do, he thought, but climb the fence, no matter the difficulties, and trust there was an open gate on the other side. The fence seemed slightly lower on the left, round-shouldered from erosion, though the far right side offered the advantage of a cement pedestal of about two feet high that might bear his weight. If he raised himself on his toes while standing on the pedestal, he could grip the fence sufficiently to pull himself over.

An old woman, banging on the sill with a shoe, called to him from the window to go away.

He waved to her, asked if there was an exit on the other side of the field.

"If you don't scoot this instant, young man, I'll have the bobbies on you," she said. She had a face that looked as if it could turn you into stone.

Terman walked away as though he had accepted her warning, not looking back until he judged himself beyond her range. The head was hanging out like a flag, peering blindly in his direction. He waited until it had withdrawn, and then a minute or so beyond that. If he could clear the fence at one jump, the unstatued pedestal his springboard, he might get by without the old lady's notice. He got a running start, had one foot over, was awkwardly split at the top, when the head thrust itself out the window and squalled at him to get away.

Her shouting harried him like a vicious dog at his heels. The second leg cleared awkwardly, ankle scraping the top. Unable to brace himself for the fall, he took all his weight on his left leg and pitched forward, his other leg folded under him like an afterthought. The pain came in flashes and seemed bearable except in moments of expectation. He was in a vacated lot, once perhaps a cricket pitch or a small park. There was the skeleton of a structure in one corner, the beginnings of an apartment complex that had either been temporarily or permanently abandoned.

He couldn't get up, reconciled himself to the arrival of the police, the inevitable nastiness and misunderstanding.

It was possible that his leg was broken, one or the other (one banged up, the other severely twisted), though he was inclined to think not. When the pain receded—the left ankle its main source—he rolled onto his side. He rested a few minutes from his exertion. Using his right arm for leverage, he gradually pulled himself upright, the preponderance of his weight on his right leg. How odd to be standing. How unnatural the position seemed. He walked a few cautious steps, putting one foot in front of the other, right first then left, then right, the process not quite as he remembered it. His body refused the upright position, longed to fall. He stopped his stuttering walk, stood with his legs apart, half-squatting, to purchase his balance. The ragged park, deserted except for an urchin kicking a soccer ball at the far end, extended itself before him. There was no sign of the police, but he could believe that the old lady would follow through on her threat. What else was there in her life? He forced himself to walk, pulling one foot, dragging the other, the space magnified by his urgency. He had to instruct his feet to get himself moving, each step ordered to specification. The far end of the park—he could make out an open gate where the boy was kicking the ball—approached him by degrees. Nausea came and went, settled in for a prolonged visit. His right foot must place itself ahead of his left and then his left must outdo, if only by several inches, if only by its own size, the presumptions of his right. The boy looked up at him, stared for a moment, then went about his business, which included a controversy with an imaginary adversary.

The closer he got to the exit—he was more than halfway there, he thought—the greater his sense of urgency. He might actually escape his pursuers, avoid confrontation with the police, find a taxi and return to the safety (the relative safety) of his own house. He didn't want to believe it, resisted hope, committed to no larger possibility than fulfilling the demands of the next step.

Only for moments did he think of the target he offered, limping slowly across the open field. It would not require a particularly good marksman to bring him down.

He was struck by the recollection of an airless Polish film he had seen in Cleveland Ohio the night of John F. Kennedy's assassination. In the movie a group of men attempt to escape the Nazis by moving through the city's sewer system, a network of underground tunnels. The maze of entrapment had never seemed more claustrophobic. One man gets through at the end. When he rises from the sewer, after having miraculously endured in that underground hell, Terman had anticipated that enemy soldiers would be waiting for him. That they weren't did not undo for him the expectation that they were there, and had chosen not to reveal themselves. The survivor redescends at the end to search for his comrades or perhaps merely because he is no longer able to bear the idea of freedom.

The right ankle becoming increasingly tender, he gradually shifted the burden of his weight from the right foot to the left. Even the present limiting circumstances yielded choices. He had to decide whether to veer from his path to pick up an old broomstick that might, if it weren't rotted out, be used as a cane.

He cut down the space between himself and the stick in short order, wanting the digression concluded and the real trip resumed. He refused to regret his choice, but a rueful feeling persisted, a sense of unredeemable error.

He squatted to acquire the warped broomstick, heard someone coming and raised his head to look, tilting backwards, restoring his balance as a trick of will. Two other boys, slightly larger than the first, had joined the urchin in his makeshift game. They were shouting at some unseen audience in mock bravado.

Terman claimed the splintery stick and rose like Lazarus to his feet.

"Hey, that's me private club," one of the newcomers yelled at him. There was some self-conscious laughter from the others.

He ignored them as a matter of choice, walked conscientiously, using the stick as a third leg, toward the open gate.

He would have liked to avoid crossing paths with the ragged soccer players, but to go out of his way was to call attention to his fear (was he even really afraid of them?), might invite some form of interference. If they decided to mug him—it could come to that without premeditation—there was little he could do to prevent it. (Where were the police the old lady had threatened to call?) He noticed another possible exit, an iron gate on the far right that was closed and possibly locked. He decided—the decision made instinctively—to continue in the direction he was going. Involved in their game, the boys might be willing to overlook his trespass.

The largest one called out to no one in particular. "That gent has got me big stick between his legs."

He thought to joke back, show them he was one of the boys himself, though held, instinct again predominating, to his decision to ignore them. The cane preceded him, step by step, had become an integral part of his act.

He passed through, had got beyond the arena of the game, without incident.

In the next moment, the ball rode by him, barely missing his leg, buckling the cane. The boys pursued the ball, were rushing helter skelter in his direction, bumping each other as they ran. The implication of the ball being kicked in his direction was hard to avoid.

They brushed him slightly as they went by (did he imagine the contact?), did him no notable damage. It might have been the wind that stroked his elbow. Was that all the harm they meant to do?

One of them, he noticed with a sideglance, was moving the ball toward him with his foot. Terman sidestepped cautiously, a delicate maneuver. The ball skipped by him.

"Goal Rangers," the boy who had been kicking it called.

They were behind him now, their movements unobservable, their loud chatter announcing the progress of the game. They played to him, their voices too loud for themselves alone, dogged his heels.

The ball again skittered past him, bounded headlong toward the open gate.

"Penalty kick," one of them called out.

He readied himself for trouble, held the cane in both hands.

In a moment they were past him, scrambling after the ball, calling to it to stop its flight. They disappeared through the open gate, pushing each other for position as they left his view, their cries of complaint hanging in the air, surviving their departure.

He felt a loss of energy like the sudden dying of a wind. Each step required more effort than its achievement seemed to warrant. He inched toward the gate, which was almost directly in front of him, his pace so slow it seemed like virtual immobility. It was curious that the soccer players hadn't returned. Terman strained to locate their voices but they were silent or had gone away. The more immediate danger became the less it frightened him.

Just as he stepped through the gate—the boys for all he knew were waiting for him on the other side—he thought of Tom hating him.

6

The truth is I had never stolen anything—maybe an occasional quarter from my mother's pocketbook—until I came to London at my father's invitation. This is not offered in defense of my behavior which I never thought of as other than indefensible. It was not even that I was driven to do what I did, though there was more than likely some element of compulsion in it. I thought of it as a game I played against myself, a game in which I forced myself to steal as a demonstration of will and a proof of competence. The pleasure, if it could be called that, was in being able to override my own resistance, which is to say I stole because I found it hateful to steal. I stole like a person writing a poem against his predilection to do something else with his time, anything else.

He was in his study when I left, Isabelle lying down in one of the second floor bedrooms. Were they looking for me? I made no serious effort to muffle my steps when I came down the stairs, expected my father to come out of his study after me, continued to expect it after I had let myself out. We're in this together, I thought.

I was walking home (or toward home, undecided on destination) when I saw him go by on Holland Park Ave. in his Ford Escort, an intense look on his face. The light turns red before he reaches the corner and he rides the brake, then races through. I watched him from the doorway of a second-hand bookstore, then followed his car for a few blocks. I had to hurry to keep the car in view, gun in jacket pocket banging against my thigh. He turned left without signalling, turned as if the decision to turn had not been made in advance.

I walked back to the second-hand bookstore, a place called Riverrun Booksellers, and looked in the glass door. A blond woman with thick-lensed glasses was sitting at a raised desk halfway back, reading a magazine. There was also an older man in the shop (her father?), but he was even farther away from the door and engrossed in some kind of inventory work. There were no other customers in the shop, which was not ideal though not necessarily disadvantageous. The woman in the glasses glanced up when I came in—a bell jingling with the opening and closing of the door—then in an unbroken gesture returned to her magazine. She didn't care.

I didn't see anything I wanted. The paperback shelves appeared to have had all the good stuff winnowed out, contained dated political tracts, old almanacs and the usual smattering of romances and mysteries, sci fi and unremembered popular fiction. I read across each shelf, starting at the top and working down, looking for a discovery or an echo, something worth the risk.

I passed it by at first, then came back to it, a title neither familiar nor unfamiliar, a book called *Out of Itself.* The title's very familiarity retarded recognition. The author's name was Terman, my own name. I thought in a hallucinatory flash that it was a book I had written myself (though of course I haven't written any books), whose existence I had stupidly forgotten.

It was my father's third novel—third or fourth—and was an edition (Panther) I'd never seen before. The blurb said, "A painful dreamlike searing work somewhere between *Malone Dies* and *The Maltese Falcon*."

Though I was momentarily unobserved, I would have liked some other people in the shop to deflect attention from me. I had the feeling that the woman at the desk was more aware of me then she pretended. The point was to disguise my intention, though I could have pocketed the book without her noticing, and I continued methodically down the shelves, stopping from time to time to look through a book I had no interest in at all.

"Is there anything in particular that you're looking for?" she asked without seeming to raise her head.

It was at the moment of her question that someone else came in the shop, announced by the bell, a tall stoop-shouldered, white-haired man, elegantly dressed.

The man walked up to the desk and asked for something in a confidential voice. He couldn't have helped more had we worked out the details of his entrance in advance.

"I've seen it around somewhere," the woman said doubtfully. "That's one of those items that's never around for long."

She wrote something down on a piece of paper and slid it across the desk to him.

My back shielding me from view, I slipped the copy of my father's book from shelf to jacket pocket while appearing to be absorbed in another book altogether.

I trembled with excitement, literally trembled. It was always that way the first few minutes I had taken something. Once I got out of the store with it, the excitement tended to pale, the stolen article without satisfaction in itself. The woman was staring at me, seemed knowing, her pursed lips tasting that knowledge. It was only suspicion I warned myself. She couldn't have seen me pocket the book. Still, there might have been something in my manner that gave me away, a guilty look, something of the kind. I smiled at her, made that effort, said I thought she had one of the nicest bookstores in London.

"Do you really?" she asked in a somewhat supercilious voice.

I nodded, turned to go, took an uneasy step toward the door, persuaded myself of my innocence. My first step was less authoritative than usual, seemed unsure of its ultimate destination.

I turned back once again, "Do you have a copy of the *Tibetan Book of the Dead*?" I asked.

"Not at the moment," she said. "Is there really such a work?"

I had my hand on the door handle.

Someone—I assumed the woman—was coming up behind me, was a step or two behind. The trick was not to panic, to behave in an ordinary way, to concern myself with the details of opening the door and stepping outside.

I had the idea of taking off her glasses, as the hero of an old-fashioned movie might do, and kissing her on the mouth.

"How you take my breath away!" she might say.

It turned out to be the man behind me, the expensively dressed white-haired man, which was not the relief I expected it to be. After I stepped out, I held the door for him which he acknowledged with an unintelligible mumble.

I went around the next corner before reaching in my jacket pocket to claim my prize. My hand was trembling again, in the throes of some self-contained desire. The tips of my fingers were close to numb.

I had been uncharacteristically careless, had stuffed the book in the pocket with the gun, making the bulge even more ostentatious than it had been.

The man who had come out of the store behind me (and had gone, I thought, in the opposite direction) was coming up the street toward me. I turned my back to him and shoved my hands in my pockets, holding the book in one of them.

He came up to me and said Hello, asked if I was an American.

I didn't deny it, though I didn't affirm it either. "Do I look like an American?"

"I heard you say something in the shop," he said, "but I recognized you as an American even before that. Incidentally, I wouldn't go back to that shop if I were you."

"You wouldn't?"

"Not if I were in your booties, young man."

He seemed too well-dressed to be a policeman, but I supposed he could be a judge or the head of Scotland Yard retired, some direct or indirect representative of the processes of retribution. I was trying to think of something to say that would justify my taking the book.

"What are you doing in London?" he asked.

It was not a question I knew how to answer. "Passing through," I said.

"Yes, that's a good answer. When I was in the states, not so long ago in point of fact, I thought of my time there in the very same choice of language." He rubbed his large hands together as if the circulation had stopped. "A bit chilly, isn't it? Rain in the air, I should guess. Summer in London is the season that never quite arrives. Why don't we go inside to continue our chat if you have no objection. I have a flat not five minutes from here or we could go to a restaurant and have some lunch."

"I don't know," I said, not sure whether I had any real choice in the matter.

My tenuous refusal caused him no apparent dismay. "Another time, shall we?" he said, taking a card from his wallet. He appeared to study the text for a few minutes before handing it over, holding it away from me for the longest possible time. "If you want someone to talk to," he said, "there's no stigma in being lonely—feel free to call me. Is that agreeable?"

I shrugged modestly, an indicaton that I didn't really understand the language he was speaking. Anything that got me away at the moment was agreeable. I half-turned to go, though waited for him to dismiss me, a good boy despite opposing evidence.

He took something from his pocket and held it in his hand so I couldn't see it. "You won't do anything foolish like that again, will you?" he said.

A shrug was the only assurance I had to offer. My eyes pleaded innocent to his veiled charge.

"I'd like you to make me that promise," he said. "Will you do that?"

"I promise I won't do anything foolish," I said in an inexpressive voice, squirming, feeling the gun in my pocket next to the book.

He laughed the way some people clear their throats. "You have renounced foolishness, have you?" he said.

I affected sincerity, which was not to say I was insincere, said unblinkingly that I had given him the promise he had asked me for.

"I don't believe you mean it," he said as if he thought my disingenuousness amusing. "Is that unfair?" His hand was in his pocket, clutching real or imaginary handcuffs.

"Who's talking about fairness?" I said, an involuntary quip, which produced a second laugh, less grudging than the first. I was warming to my audience.

We walked two blocks together, though I wasn't sure who was going in whose direction, during which time he gave me a lecture on what I assumed to be the disadvantages of shop-lifting. Yet he was so oblique in his approach I couldn't be sure that he wasn't alluding to something else altogether.

All of the time we walked—his purposes as obscure to me as his conversation—I wanted nothing more than to get away from him.

"I have to go," I suddenly blurted out.

"Which way?" he asked.

There was of course no place at which I was expected, though I gave him a story about being interviewed for a job as an usher at a West End theater.

"What time do you have to be there?" he asked.

Thinking that it was about ten thirty, I said without hesitation that I had to be at the theater at eleven o'clock.

He laughed, put his arm on my shoulder. "You've already missed that appointment. Come, let's go into a restaurant and have some lunch. It might be I know the chap you're supposed to meet and can arrange another appointment for you." He led me, his hand on my back steering me along, to an Italian restaurant called Mama Lucia. I went with him merely because it was easier than resisting. The truth was I was hungry (I hadn't eaten breakfast and perhaps not even dinner the night before) and the old gentleman seemed to have more money than he knew how to spend.

When the menu came I had difficulty locating something I wanted. I professed to have no appetite.

"Let me order for you," said my patron. "I know the kind of thing they do best."

He ordered for us both, ordered in Italian so I had a vague and mostly mistaken notion of what he had chosen for me. I hadn't wholly relinquished the idea that he had taken me in custody (was this my last meal?) for the theft of my father's book. At the same time, it was clear to me I was free to get up and leave if the impulse took me.

At the outset, before we had been seated, there was difficulty about my wearing my jacket (my thrift shop U.S. Army field jacket) to the table, my host suggesting that I give it to the checkroom girl. But I said I never took it off, a remark he seemed to enjoy, clearing his odd laugh from his throat.

I felt my assertion of not being hungry, which was only true the moment before it was spoken, as an obligation to self-denial. I withheld appetite, picked over my food with hard-earned indifference.

I had never been into wine, though dutifully drank whatever was put in my glass. We had red wine with the antipasto and white wine with the main dish, which was some unidentifiable meat stuffed with creamed spinach and some relative of ham.

The wine affected me like an anesthetic. The more I drank the more paralyzed I got, my conversation reducing itself to mumbles and asides.

I was supposed to be funny—it was his idea of me—and I did what I could to sustain an overrated reputation.

"If you're really interested in a job," he said at some point, "maybe I could do something for you."

"As long as it doesn't require killing anyone," I said, a remark that struck me as extremely amusing when I made it. I laughed nervously to cover the pall of his silence.

"So you draw the line at murder, do you?" he said. "One ought to draw the line somewhere, I suppose."

"I'm very good at drawing lines and waiting on queues," I said. This idiocy provoked a small, disheartened laugh from my patron.

For no reason I could say, I was cutting the meat on my plate in microscopic pieces. It took ten mouthfuls, I estimated, to achieve an ordinary two or three. My host tried not to notice or not to seem to notice.

A second bottle of white wine was uncorked and my glass refilled. I emptied the glass as if it were medicine, persuaded in my sodden state that the gesture was amusing to my audience.

I could imagine the grotesque impression I was making, though couldn't stop what I was doing, had no clear idea what it was. The job was not mentioned again in the next few minutes and I was willing to believe my host had reconsidered his offer. Just when I thought I had offended him beyond repair he handed me his card and said I was to call him whenever I was ready. Meaning ready to go to work? I didn't ask.

I found myself calling him sir—I put the card away without reading his name—and thought that was wrong somehow (my voice had a satirical edge), though he seemed to have no objection. He called me sir in return and occasionally son. I couldn't remember if I mentioned my name to him or even if he had asked for it. I don't think anything I told him was precisely the truth.

"Will you have some dessert, son?" he asked.

I was still working at the meat, picking at it like a sore. "I don't think so, sir," I said, a parody of the polite young man. "I never know what I want until after I've had it."

My host lit a cigar, glanced at his watch, drummed his fingers on the table. There was a hum of impatience in his manner, a feeling of disappointment. I knew it like the back of my hand. He felt he had made a mistake in taking me to lunch and was anxious to get on to something else.

I asked him what he did, what kind of work if any.

He waved the question away as if it were the smoke from someone else's cigar. "I do what needs doing," he said. The waiter, who may have also been the owner, shadowed my plate, waiting for me to turn my head.

The veal—I had become confident of its identity—had long since turned chilly, though I had some stake, or thought I had, in eating a few more pieces, a way of nullifying the effects of the wine.

"He's finished," my host said in the manner of a man who knew the gods by their first names. The waiter gave a sigh of relief and cleared my plate.

I mourned the loss of my uneaten meal. That was no way to treat a guest, I thought.

"Will there be anything else, gentlemen?" the waiter asked.

"Just the bill thank you," said my host, filling my glass with what remained of the second bottle of white wine.

I drank slowly this time, pretending to savor the wine I could no longer really taste.

I caught his glance when I looked up. He seemed to be studying me. "What kind of job did you have in mind?" I asked. I yawned, felt weighted with tiredness.

The old gentleman asked with undisguised distaste if I was going to be sick—my head was on the table or close enough to it to offer that suspicion—and I heard myself answer, "Wouldn't think of it."

He raised himself to his full height, paid the check and seemed to leave the restaurant, but then he was standing over me again. I had the idea he had gone around in a revolving door. "I can't leave you here like this, son," he said.

He held out his hand and when I realized what he had in mind, I took hold and rose to my feet. Muffling a belch, I preceded him in a snaky line to the door. The waiter, who seemed to have nothing better to do, followed in our wake, forming a small procession. He was carrying something on a plate and it struck me that it was my gun, that it had fallen from my jacket and he had rescued it. "Where's he going with that?" I asked the old man. Then, wanting to make sure of things, I shoved my hand in my pocket and brought out the gun for the briefest of airings, my father's novel dislodged in the process. The gun had been there all the time.

When I recovered the book I stuffed it in a different pocket of my field jacket. There were some shocked glances in the restaurant but no direct mention was made of the pistol. What could my host have possibly thought? I offered neither acknowledgement nor explanation.

#

"You have a visitor," the landlady said the moment I came through the door.

I never thought to ask who it was, went up the stairs carrying Mrs. Chepstow's eyes on my back. My pockets were stuffed with the day's loot.

I called down to her. "Mrs. C, I don't want anyone in my room when I'm not there."

The woman sidestepped complaints like a halfback, seemed able to disappear through one door or another at whim.

The door to my room was shut and I knocked at it before entering, my other hand embracing the gun in my pocket.

My visitor—it was odd how I mistook who it was—got up from my bed and poked her head forward to kiss me on the cheek. It was Astrid not Isabelle. She looked radiant and I almost supposed myself the occasion for it. The room—I hadn't noticed it at first—had been fixed up a bit; there were yellow flowers in a blue vase on the rickety end table. My dirty clothes, mostly underwear and socks, had been moved into some discreet obscurity. It was not what I wanted, the improved-upon squalor, but I thanked her for her pains. She had appropriated the bed and I sat down in the room's one chair which she had moved from one odd corner to another in an excess of zeal. The room was no less ugly for having been improved, its full-blown tackiness compromised by genteel aspiration.

I looked around the room and wondered how anyone who didn't hate himself could live in it, then I walked around as I sometimes do when I'm alone.

She winked at me from my bed, her hands behind her head, asked if she was keeping me from doing something I had to do.

The entire room took on the scent of her perfume, its own peculiar anonymity. Was I wrong in thinking she was wearing more of it than usual? I wanted her gone, though also felt rewarded by her uninvited visit.

I apologized for the meagerness of the room, said sometimes it grows on you. Sometimes not.

"I think it's cozy," she said in a breathy voice, moistening her lips with her tongue.

There was almost nothing she could do to rouse me in my present mood. I was indifferent to the taut outline of her birdlike breasts, the lacy hem of her slip, the thin pale thighs.

"You seem to be miles away, Tommy," she said. "In which direction are you traveling?"

I heard, or thought I did, somone's heavy foot on the stairs and put my ear to the door to listen. Astrid sat up and smoothed her short skirt over her knees.

"What is it, Tommy?" she asked, hugging her knees. To entertain my guest, perhaps to frighten her too, I took out my father's gun and stood behind the door, waiting for whoever it was to try to force his way in. I wondered what I would really do if the door swung open. Astrid giggled, put her hand over her mouth.

The playacting began to depress me and I returned the gun to my pocket. I continued to sense that someone was there just beyond the door (Mrs. Chepstow or my father), positioned to eavesdrop, standing absolutely still to avoid discovery.

Astrid tiptoed over, felt the outline of the gun against my side. Her question was unspoken.

When we were outside, walking in the dreary rain, I was sorry I hadn't gone to bed with her. I held her narrow hand as we walked.

"You're nicer now," she whispered to me.

She was wearing (why hadn't I noticed before?) the scarf I had given her, a flowery thing I had picked up at Liberty's in one of my earliest forays. I complimented her on it, though in fact it seemed to overwhelm her face.

"When are you going to introduce me to your father?" Astrid asked. We, in fact, seemed to be walking in that direction.

I suggested we go to Soho, the idea arriving the moment I announced it.

"If you want to Tommy," she said, all acquiescence and self-denial. If I were capable of believing anything, I would have believed at that moment that she imagined herself in love with me.

The cruelty of my mood resisted compromise. There wasn't a passing figure in the street for whom I didn't have an unexpressed contempt. I raged at the bus for taking so long to arrive, all the time pretending it didn't matter, pretending to an almost catatonic self-control. Astrid held on to my arm, chattered.

The 77 Bus finally came (two others of its kind in close succession), and we went, at my insistence, to the upper level. It was crowded and we had to take seats on the aisle behind one another. As soon as we were seated, Astrid clutched my arm, whispered something I was not prepared to hear.

Someone she didn't want to see was on the same bus, Astrid in a panic.

She looked around to see who else might be listening, then pursed her mouth to my ear, "It's the man I've been going with."

I waited for the import of this discovery to sound itself, but Astrid had nothing more to say at that moment. Each time the bus stopped she looked out the window to see if he had gotten off.

Later I learned, or am I making it up, I'm never sure, that the man was married and almost twice her age and that she had been sleeping with him since she was sixteen.

The woman next to her got up and Astrid took the window seat and I moved into the vacated seat alongside her. Everything had changed. "Why do you care if he sees you?" I asked.

"I just don't want him to," she snapped. "That's enough reason, isn't it?"

Stop after stop she stared anxiously out the window, her head drawn back, wanting to see without being seen. He didn't get off, or she didn't see him get off, his (real or imagined) presence barring our way.

I mentioned that it wasn't possible to see everyone who got off at every stop.

I tried to amuse her but I was in no mood to be amusing . "I'll plug him for you," I said.

She looked at me in alarm, shocked or frightened. After we turned the corner at Oxford Circus she got up without a word and made her way to the stairs in back. I waited to the last possible moment before following.

The streets were mobbed, tourists packed three and four deep, not everyone moving in the same direction. I thought I saw Astrid just ahead of me when I stepped off the bus, but before I could get to her she had merged with the crowd.

It didn't strike me at first that it had been her intention to lose me. Only afterward when I had pushed my way through the mob did I recognize the obvious and even then it was not easy to accept. I called her name once, shouted it in a voice that might have made her wince had she heard me. Once seemed sufficient. She had gone off, I had to believe, with the other guy. It was like a recapitulation of everything in my life, so I had no business being surprised or hurt.

I stood on my toes, observing and I suppose being observed, then I joined the human race and let it take me where it was going. I took my revenge in indifference.

#

Later in the day, I thought I saw Astrid from the back walking with a man that could have been my father. When I got closer I saw it was two other people, and I began to wonder how much of what I saw was real and how much hallucinatory. Perhaps I hadn't yet arrived in London, perhaps I was on the plane coming over and had imagined what might happen when I got to London, or perhaps I hadn't yet boarded the plane and was in my bed at home thinking of the trip.

7

He thought it odd that Isabelle hadn't answered the phone, tried to imagine where she might have gone, was angry at her defection. A taxi went by, was gone before he could call to it, before he could step from the booth and make himself known. Through the glass of the phone box, the street, the one he had come to through the small park, gave off glints of familiarity. He had visited it before, perhaps earlier that day. The peeling facade of a yellowish frame house directly across from where he stood had been a point on some trip he had once taken or dreamed.

He had the idea that Isabelle, worried about his prolonged absence, had gone out to search for him, had taken a bus or taxi to his son's apartment with certain disastrous consequences.

He also had the idea (one didn't cancel out the other) that Max Kirstner had arrived at his house and finding Isabelle alone, had persuaded her to go off with him to his flat in South Kensington. It was no less possible that she was in the shower or had gone to work.

In five minutes, or ten (or twenty-five), he was at his car, was in the driver's seat, his head against the steering wheel. He didn't have to raise his head to notice that there were three men across the street, staring at him, one of them the devious Pakistani that had dogged his steps.

Terman started up the car, considering only briefly what options remained to him if it didn't start. All the while, a mist of rain coming through the half-opened window, he sweated from some private heat. He imagined himself taking a hot bath, a recuperative bath, soaking his swollen ankle, washing the sweat from his face. It was better than any real bath might have been, this imagination of bath, calmed his terrors.

He drove home, sat in the car for no time at all after he parked, felt incapable of letting himself out, of crossing the street, of unlocking the door to his house.

A furious woman, unimaginably familiar, was tapping at the window with a key.

"Didn't you see me?" she was asking. "I was standing at the entrance to the park when you drove by and I was calling you, wasn't I, and waving my arms."

Isabelle came around and got in the other side of the car, though neither of them was going anywhere. "Tell my about it," she said. "Did it go all right?"

He misjudged her sympathy and tried to kiss her on the neck, the collar of her blouse obstructing his intent. She pushed him away, using all her strength, drove him into the handle of his own door.

Later, after he had taken his hot bath and gone to bed, she tiptoed into the room and apologized for having been so upset with him. Terman feigned sleep, feigned dreams, feigned dying.

She cuddled his head against her chest or he dreamed her doing it.

He imagined or dreamed, imagined he dreamed or dreamed he imagined, the following conversation.

"I never got to see him."

"That's odd, isn't it? You were gone such a long time I thought surely you were with him."

"I ran into difficulty, a series of difficulties. I was going to call you and tell you about it but I couldn't find a public phone and when I did and called you there was no answer."

She was holding his hand to her mouth (or so he imagined) when the phone interrupted. "Why don't we let it pass," he dreamed himself saying.

Isabelle left to answer the phone while Terman imagined that he was the one that had gotten out of bed to confront the unknown. Isabelle said Hallo. Max was on the line to announce he was flying to Los Angeles in the morning. Isabelle said Hallo, the sound returning like an echo from a distant place.

She shouted something unintelligible, her voice unusually shrill, then hung up the phone.

Isabelle waited for him to ask what happened before committing her story to him. As it was, he had no intention of asking. Her experience with the silent phone went unshared.

A second phone call seemed to wake him several hours later and he picked up the receiver to hear Max do his well-worn imitation of English fatuity.

"BBC here," he said. "Not disturbing anything, old boy, am I?

We're all wild over here about televiewing the story of your life if you could condense it into five or six absolutely smashing words."

"I think you have the wrong number," Terman said.

"This isn't the brilliant, Dr. T? I'd know that voice anywhere, luv."

"Dr. T done gone away," he said.

"When you see the scoundrel, old boy, might you tell him that Max Kirstner will be in California for the next half week, some business to transact. The international director will be appearing on the show, Let's Make a Deal."

"Don't expect ever to see that man, boss."

"If you do run into the old boy, tell him that Max liked what he read of his latest rewrites, liked but not loved, though he is willing to compromise on matters of the heart. To keep up the good work and all that. Ciao, bambino."

Terman called to Isabelle and got no answer, merely the return of her name, the echo of her absence.

When he found himself fully awake it was about midnight, he guessed, though it could have been any time. Days might have passed, whole lifetimes. A woman was asleep next to him, one of her legs curling about his like a vine.

He woke hungry and went downstairs in the dark to fix himself something to eat, the sore ankle still somewhat tender, though vastly improved for its rest.

The sleep had refreshed him—he was maneuvering down the stairs in the dark—and he considered that he was having, or had had, a condition known as breakdown.

He felt remarkably good at this moment of reckoning, felt like whistling or making love or watching an old American movie on television, preferably a western or mystery.

The house was absolutely dark, was dark the way a religious mystery is dark; it was illumined by dark.

The chairs in the large parlor were occupied by shadows. He saluted them as he passed, raising two fingers to his forehead, a gesture out of some other time or place. The shadows ignored his passage or took it for granted.

He was in the kitchen, had found his way there without turning on a single light, and was standing in front of the refrigerator.

He was on the steps coming down, his ankle paining him, holding on to the bannister as he made his way.

He poured himself a congnac, sat down on the maroon velvet couch in the large parlor and adjusted his eyes to the nuances of blackness.

He took a slice of baked ham from the refrigerator and made an open sandwich with it on a thick slice of stale black bread. He took a bite out of it then decided it wasn't what he wanted and returned to the large parlor without it. His son Tom was waiting there for him.

He came down the stairs with both hands on the bannister, each step a plunge into the unimaginable. They had the following conversation.

"Is that you, Dad?" one of the shadows asked him. "I understand you've been looking for me."

"I may have been. I don't remember."

"You don't remember that you drove down from Ramsgate or Kent or whatever to say something to me that couldn't wait?"

"It's true that Isabelle and I drove down from Ramsgate through the night."

"In the morning you got into your car—I don't know if it's yours or if it's a rented job—and went looking for me."

"The fact remains, and I think we ought to stay close to the facts, the fact remains that I didn't find you."

"Let me get this straight, Dad, okay? You're denying that you were looking for me at all. It was coincidental that you were flashing around in my neighborhood and lost your way."

"No. What I'm saying is this. The outcome of an act more or less defines its intention. I may have been looking for you or thought that that's what I was about, but there's no evidence that I actually wanted to find you."

"It's about time you admitted it," Tom said.

An uneasy quiet followed, in which Terman got up and walked about.

"Is there something you want to say to me, Tom?" he asked.

Tom shook his head or so it appeared in the dark room. The abrupt movement of a shadow, dark against dark, darker against darker.

"Do you have the pistol with you?" Terman asked.

"With me?"

"I'd like to have it back if you don't mind."

"It's in the pocket of my jacket. I take it with me everywhere."

"I appreciate that," Terman said under his breath. "Still, if you don't mind, I'd like to have it back."

"Do you need it right away, Dad? If you don't, I'd like to , you know, hold onto it a while longer."

Terman held out his hand, which was invisible in the dark room. "It's out of the question," he said. "What did you want it for in the first place?"

"I had nothing, you know, in mind. I just liked having it, just liked the idea of having it with me. Do you know what I mean? It was there for me."

The same question kept returning. "There to do what with?"

"To do whatever. I mean, what use did you have for it?"

"The hero of the movie I was writing carried one and I acquired the gun as a form of research."

"Yeah," Tom said. "Right. If our reasons weren't exactly the same, they weren't so different either. Did you ever get to shoot it?"

The shadow leaned forward to ask the last question, the question pulling him forward.

"I went to a shooting range once," Terman said. "It was a place for members only but Max knew the people in charge and so got us access. They had silhouettes of people and if you hit one in a vital part it would keel over."

Tom laughed nervously. "Did you get off on it, Dad?"

"It was like eating forbidden fruit, had that fascination. Still, we were only playing."

"You were doing research, right?"

"Are you being ironic with me?"

"If I am, it wasn't intentional," said the disingenuous shadow. "Do you think I was being ironic, Dad?"

The smarmy sincerity was more offensive to him than the irony, though he choked back his disapproval.

"I'm really sorry if it sounded that way," Tom said. "Forget it, okay?"

"Perhaps I'm being over-sensitive or projecting my own view of myself on to you."

"Let it go," Tom whispered.

"I accept your version of it," Terman said in a voice that engendered irony in his own ear.

"You may have been right about my tone," confided the shadow. "I have a hard time—other people have told me this—letting people be the way they are. My mother says I disapprove of everything."

"Does she?"

"Hey, who's being ironic now?" He laughed goodnaturedly. "Anyway she didn't really say that. I like to attribute my own perceptions to others. It gives them the voice of authority."

Again Terman held his hand out in ambiguous demand. "I think it would be a good idea, Tom, if you gave me back the gun."

"You don't have to keep after me about it," said the shadow. "Anyway, there are a few things I want to get off my chest first.'"

"Do you want to tell me for the hundredth time that I'm a disappointment to you?" The subject was sore to him, a perpetually reopened wound, and he regretted advancing it. What was this conversation about anyway?

"You could at least hear me out," the shadow said harshly, "before you tell me I've nothing to say to you."

"It's no pleasure to me to be told once again that I've disappointed you. If you have something else to say, something that adds to the store of knowledge between us, I'll listen to that."

The shadow laughed, then lapsed into silence. He stammered something.

"What?"

"It wasn't your pleasure I was thinking of,"he said. "It's my recollection, okay?, that I never told you what was really getting to me. I never told you because I was afraid to. Even now in the dark where we can't even see each other's face, I can't get a fucking word out." The news Terman awaited was like a delayed time bomb. His only escape was to run from the house and keep running.

Tom seemed on the verge of speaking, but nothing was said.

"Would it satisfy you if I apologized in advance?" Terman asked. "I'm terribly sorry I've failed you." He stood up as if the couch had suddenly released him. "What the hell do you want from me?" Tom said nothing. Terman said he was sorry he had shouted and sat down.

#

"I hear you want me to go back to New York," Tom said after a prolonged silence.

Terman resisted inquiring into the source of Tom's information, though couldn't imagine how the news had come to him indirectly. "That was one of the things I wanted to say to you," he said. "The reason is self-evident."

"Yeah," he said, the word barely leaving his mouth. "I remember a time in California when I was supposed to stay with you for three weeks and, for some reason never explained to me, I was sent home in disgrace after five days. I remembered that for a long time."

"I don't remember it at all," Terman said. "This happened in California? Are you sure it was California?"

The recollection came supported by a wealth of corroborating detail. The color and texture of a couch in the living room of a rented cottage. The insufficient room in the back where he was made to stay, a place with grease-stained yellow walls and infested spider webs, the floor made of dirt. Lizards darted across the ceiling at night like dismembered fingers. A blond girl in braids named Alma who liked to sunbathe nude on the terrace stayed with them.

"What did I do that you had to send me away?" Tom asked.

"I never lived with a woman named Alma," Terman said.

"I remember the two of you talking about me one night after I was supposed to be asleep," Tom said. "You were both complaining at how I made things difficult for you, was always underfoot or something. 'Snooping' was the word Alma used. The kid is always snooping around, she said, and you did nothing to dissuade her of the notion that I was this mutt you had taken in off the street that had shat on the rug without permission."

"You're making that up," Terman said, smiling in the dark despite the tightening in his chest the conversation had caused him.

"I stayed awake the whole night," said the shadow, "unable to get out of my head the creepy picture of myself the two of you had given me. I remember, though I was totally depressed, that I didn't cry. I realized, you know, that I didn't need to cry, that I used to do it to attract sympathy and I was beyond that. I didn't want to trivialize my pain by making a public demonstration of it. A couple of days after that you told me I was flying back the next morning, that you had called my mother and that she would be at the airport to pick me up."

False memories, like happy marriages, are all alike, he was tempted to say. Instead, he offered an alternative version of the event as a gesture of melioration. "What I think may have happened," he said, "is that, feeling rejected, you asked to go home and then when I acquiesced to your wishes, you made it out that I was the one sending you away."

"I don't think so, I really don't, but it comes to the same thing. Why did I feel I had done something wrong?"

The period in California seemed more like a movie he had slept through and reinvented than something real in his life. A small time producer named Godowitz had flown him out to do a screenplay of his second novel, *Out of Itself,* and he stayed on in the sun, chasing elusive gold for almost two years, one aborted project leading to another. He made some money and lost some time, picked up a screen credit for what turned out to be a single surviving line of dialogue. Tom and Kate's visits during this period were as shadowy to him as the rest of the experience. The odd thing was, the oddest thing, was that he had no recollection of ever having lived with a woman named Alma. "Are you positive the woman's name was Alma?" he asked. His memory never used to be so poor.

"I have the idea she was astoundingly young," said Tom. "Like sixteen. And she never wore shoes. She had this pair of orange sneakers that she wore around her neck with the laces tied together."

"Not possible," he said. If there was someone like that, some barefooted sixteen year old hippie who in some moment of distraction he had allowed to move in with him, her name at least was something else. He closed his eyes, worked at recovering the forgotten name of a woman he couldn't believe he had ever known.

"When the fog lifted which was like once a week," the shadow said, "you could see the water from the window of my room. Each time it appeared it was like some kind of miracle. Alma used to come in, I remember this very clearly, and stare at the ocean from my window. She said she was a water sign which meant looking into the water was like looking into herself."

"There never was an Alma in my life," Terman said.

The shadow across from him let out its breath in a staccato of disappointments.

"I didn't mean to upset you," Terman said. "It may be that your memory of that period is more accurate than mine. I concede that much."

"Do you?" he asked. "What if there were a gun to your head, what would you say?"

"Whose gun are you thinking of putting to my head?"

"It was just a figure of speech, for God's sake. You don't have to be so literal about it."

"It's only a figure of speech when you don't have a gun in your possession. I'll ask you to give it back to me one last time."

"Or what?"

"Is that the way you want it?" Terman asked.

"It's the way you want it." The voice childish, pained.

He thought to ask again for the return of the gun, but decided that further reiteration would only weaken the impact of his request. He was on the verge of saying something unforgivable. "I'll never forgive you for this," he said. Abruptly it came to him, the recollection interrupting the flow of his anger. "The girl's name was Opal, the one with the braids around her head. She was very odd, had been living in an abandoned car on the beach before moving in with me. She was beautiful and profoundly remote. I took her vagueness for some kind of mystery."

"I still remember her as Alma," said the other. "She had the thinnest lips of anyone I'd ever seen."

At some point the conversation began to repeat itself.

"I had no expectations in regard to this visit," Tom said. "My mother said she thought it would be an educational experience for me."

"She thought that visiting you father would be an educational experience?"

"That visiting London would be. You make a gesture and then you never follow through on it. It's okay. I mean, it no longer comes as a surprise to me. I don't expect anything from you any more so you can't disappoint me."

"I think it would be best it you went home in a few days," Terman said.

"If that's what you want. You once told me, though I doubt you'd remember, that any place you were living was also my home."

"I remember."

"It doesn't hold any more, right? Or you never meant it in the first place?"

At some point the conversation among shadows came full circle. Terman came down the steps in the dark with both hands on the bannister, each step a plunge into the unimaginable.

"I understand you've been looking for me," a disembodied voice announced.

"I may have been. I don't remember."

#

A middle-aged man in a dressing gown is looking at his face in the wall mirror of an oversized bathroom. He rubs the back of his hand across his cheek, decides he needs a shave, is putting lather on his face when the phone rings. He considers not answering but after several rings picks up the phone which is on a marble table next to the toilet and says, "Monsieur Lange ici."

"This is Henry Berger," the voice says. "A mutual friend gave me your number."

"Pardon."

"I understand that you spoke English."

"Not so good I'm afraid. What may I do for you, Mr. Barber?" *He takes the receiver with him to the mirror and continues lathering his face.*

"Is there anyone in the house with you?"

"Pardon, monsieur. I fail to understand."

"Monsieur Lange, I'll say this as plainly as I can. I have a strong reason to believe that your life may be in immediate danger." *Monsieur Lange looks at the razor in his hand, then puts it down as if distrustful even of himself.* "And how do you know such things if it is not youself who is the assassin?"

We cut to Henry Berger, who is calling from a phone booth in front of a service station. "It is possible," *he says,* "that the assasssin is someone you know, someone you may even trust."

Monsieur Lange resumes shaving. "Quite alarming," *he says with some irony.* "Have you notified the police, Monsieur Becker? Do you not think the police ought to be informed of so serious a matter?"

"I can understand your skepticism. A man you don't know calls you in the middle of the night to tell you your life is in danger. Why should you believe him? Still, there's no harm in taking precautions, is there? One of the precautions I would have you take is not to stand near a window, at least not so your silhouette is revealed to someone watching outside. And another is not to inform the local police."

Lange turns the light out in the bathroom. "You are either mad, my friend, or have been given misinformation. There's nobody who wishes me evil. Now I think it is time to say goodnight."

"Your name was found in a certain notebook among other names," Berger says quickly. "You know what I'm talking about. The men whose names were on the list above yours, all except two, have died under what the police call suspicious circumstances."

M. Lange lights a cigarette and sits down on the commode. "So it follows that I'm to be rubbed out next. Yes? I promise to be wary of every suspicious sound, Monsieur Barber. Now if you'll excuse me." *M. Lange hangs up the phone abruptly. After putting out the cigarette and turning on the light, he returns to the mirror to shave the left side of his face. While he is shaving he hears footsteps outside or perhaps from another part of the house. He puts down the razor and goes to the phone, checking first to see that the bathroom door is locked from the inside.*

M. Lange phones the Chief of Police, mentions the call from Henry Berger. As they talk, we cut to Henry Berger driving through the woods presumably toward M. Lange's estate.

Standing in the dark, M. Lange listens for footsteps and hears none. He puts the light on and continues shaving. He studies his aristocratic face in the mirror, admiring his profile, distressed by the blemishes, the inevitable demarcations of age. He salutes himself, one formidable figure to another. At that moment, he hears a crash as if something, a vase perhaps, had been knocked off a table. "Merde," he whispers. The faint footsteps resume and he concentrates on them, trying to determine if they are from within the house or outside. He looks at his watch. Perhaps it is someone he knows, his son returned or one of the servants.

"C'est toi, Jacques?" he calls.

There is no answer. He looks at his watch again. The footsteps have stopped and he waits for them to renew, then goes to the phone and calls the Chief of Police a second time. "My men should be there at any moment," the Inspector says. *Abruptly the doorbell rings.* "I'm not going to hang up," Lange says.

"Hold on until I get back." *Lange puts on a shirt, brushes his hair, then lets himself out of the bathroom. He goes warily down a long corridor toward the front door, announcing himself in a loud voice. There is another corridor, then a small foyer to pass through.* "Un moment," he calls, dismayed that the police haven't rung a second time.

When Lange gets to the front door he has some difficulty unlatching it, pressured by panic. He is again in control of himself, all icy dignity, as he opens the door to confront a figure in a ski mask, holding a gun. Two shots are fired point blank before M. Lange can protest and he stumbles back into the cavernous house. He plunges into a sitting room, trailed by his own blood. He collapses, then revives and pulls himself laboriously toward a phone, knocking over a Chinese vase in his path.

"Je suis assassiné," he says into the phone, dragging it off the table as he falls.

#

Sunlight was in his eyes when Terman got up from the couch, unaware of the date or time of day. The kitchen cupboard was even barer than he anticipated, as if rats or thieves had been there first. There was nothing to satisfy his hunger in this borrowed house, the refrigerator and cupboards seeming to empty of themselves.

He remembered putting certain things away, remembered carrying a box of groceries in his arms, a pint of milk, box of tea, six croissants, half dozen brown eggs, bottle of claret, package of McVittie's digestives, jar of Wilkinson's raspberry conserves. He tended to shop as need demanded, rarely bringing in provisions with anything but the forthcoming meal in mind. Still, nothing, nothing at all, had survived the night.

"You've been behaving like a mad person," Isabelle said, "do you know?"

"The madness is unintentional," he said, meaning it as an apology. He was looking in a parlor closet for a walking stick he was postive he had seen in there, riffling among boots and umbrellas.

"Terman, I'm very unhappy with you," she said. "I'm going into work in a few minutes and I wanted to say that."

"Why isn't anything where it was?" he asked. He held out his hand to her.

"Am I invisible?" she asked him. "Once in a while you fix on me and then you pay me some attention, but I could be an inanimate object for all that." Her hand in his was like a trapped mouse. "That's all I have to say."

"I don't dispute it,' he said.

She looked up at his face, wary of unheard irony, angry at him beyond respite. He stood with his head down, took his scolding like a child. "I have to go now," she said, kissing the side of his head. She extracted her hand. "I don't know that I'll be back this evening. Do you want me to ring up if I change my mind?"

"I can understand that you might want to be alone," he said, meaning to be polite or generous.

She didn't say anything to that. The unspoken comment was sufficient, she thought.

He nodded his assent, though his agreement had not been requested. It was not that she was invisible to him as she said, but that the whole physical world was vanishing by degrees before his eyes.

There was something she felt she had to tell him before she left, she said, trying to underplay the melodrama of such a statement. She had an actress's ability to maintain her self-possession while undergoing storms of distress or anxiety. It was when her manner was most glacial that those who could read her knew she was most deeply upset. Terman, it might be said, saw nothing, not even the contemptuous manner she wore like a mask. His distraction was complete.

The confession came and went, untempered by regret. She had gone off with Max Kirstner that afternoon he had stayed behind to work on the screenplay. It was a gesture, she supposed, more self-defeating than spiteful, though for which she had no intention of apologizing. "It's out of character for me to behave that way," she said, "so I tend to blame you for it. I feel, isn't it odd, that you were the one that betrayed me."

Her accusation seemed neither to hit the mark nor miss it altogether and he accepted it as he had the report of her liaison with Max.

"Get the hell out of here," he said suddenly angry. He opened the door and pushed her out.

The conversation continued briefly after she had gone, completed itself. "Perhaps I'll be back the day after," she said.

"Perhaps you will," he said.

A few minutes later he was on the telephone in a response to a ringing that went on beyond its course.

"Hello," he said, leaning jauntily on an umbrella as if he thought he might be Fred Astaire.

There was a click on the other end. He knew who it was, had gotten the message.

He couldn't remember if he had gone shopping or had only thought about going, had lived through the anticipation of it, and so checked the refrigerator and cupboards again.

When he returned from the store with a box of groceries—the weight of his arms presented itself as evidence—the phone was ringing again.

"Marjorie Kirstner here," the voice said.

He had expected the click again, the knife edge of disconnection, or indeed something worse. "Where are you calling from?" he asked.

"I'm in London," she said. "I'm staying with some friends." He heard symphonic music in the background and a counterpoint of voices: someone was laughing or crying. "If you're not too busy, perhaps we could meet for tea this afternoon."

It was as if his memory were getting shorter and shorter so that as soon as a moment had passed it was already lost to him. "Who is this?" he asked.

She laughed, took the question—how else might it be taken?—as as uninspired joke. "It's Marjorie, darling," she said. "You haven't forgotten already, I hope."

"Do you want to come here?" he asked. "Is that why you called?"

She was silent for a moment and he thought he heard a click, terrible and decisive, within the silence. The voice returned, altered by the expedition. "Do you really mean that?" it asked. "I can't think that it would be appropriate."

He tapped the umbrella on the floor to the tune of an American song called "Nature Boy," which he hadn't heard or even thought of hearing for twenty-five years.

"Is there someone there with you?" she asked.

"Where with me?"

"At your house, Terman. Isn't that what we're talking about, luv?"

"We're talking about love," he said. "Isn't that what we're talking about?"

"Are you being nasty with me," she asked, "or has there been a genuine misunderstanding?"

He said he couldn't remember which, his memory failing, which made her laugh her odd tinkling laugh.

"What's your pleasure, luv?" she said. "Should I come chez tu or would you rather meet on the town?"

Some time later in the day, when it was getting to be four o'clock in the afternoon, the doorbell sounded. Terman had been in the study when interrupted, holding conversations with the detective Henry Berger.

When he opened the massive door—he thought of the house sometimes as an enormous vault—standing there was a woman about his own age and an elegant young man who seemed not much older than his son.

"You've met Emile, I believe," Marjorie said.

Marjorie sent the aging young man on a tour of the house—she herself had been in all its corners when her husband had used it as a location for his film, "Ceremony of Night"—and went with Terman into the kitchen for some private conversation.

"Where is your adorable friend?" she asked in a confidential voice, taking his arm. "Are you two no longer a thing, as they say in America?"

He could think of no answer to make, felt at once bereft and unencumbered.

"I expect our situations have quelque chose in common," she whispered, inclining her head toward him.

"How's that?" he roused himself to ask.

It was the right question, but she indicated with a rolling of her eyes that she had no intention of answering. "Max has gone to California for a few days," she said, "and I'm rather at loose ends. We were in the middle of a fight that had to be postponed indefinitely."

He was thinking that Max had all but given up on the Henry Berger film and that Marjorie had come, in Max's absence, to break the news to him.

"It's still in consideration," she said. "Don't think it isn't, luv. I don't remember what I may have said but I suspect I was being a bit bitchy whatever it was. You'll forgive me, won't you?"

Henry Berger was almost always a step or two behind the conspiracy, finding corpses wherever he went, pursuing ominous implications.

"Truth to tell, I came to ask your advice," she said. "I am in grave need of a bit of wisdom if you don't mind."

Terman laughed until his sides hurt, until tears broke from his eyes. "What wisdom can I give you?"

Emile floated into the kitchen and sat down at the head of the table, had the air of studying his own reflection in an imaginary mirror.

Marjorie said something to him in French and the aging child pouted in parody of grievance and turned his chair around. She winked at Terman. Her life with Max was a melodrama of betrayal and abuse, she confided in the presence of Emile's impassive back. What should she do? What would he do it he were in a similar bind?

"You will never leave him," Emile said with barely the trace of an accent.

"I will. I will," she said with exaggerated passion. Her manner included an awareness of self-parody.

They had their tea—Marjorie had brought cream cakes from Fortnum and Mason—in the large gloomy kitchen. There was a scene like it in the movie, "Ceremony of Night"—two men and a woman having tea in that very kitchen, one the woman's stepfather, the other her lover.

Henry Berger is aware as he enters the Florentine villa that he has been set up by his own people, has been marked for assassination. What he doesn't know is that a friend and former colleague is the intended assassin.

At some point Emile departed the kitchen on some unannounced mission. Marjorie took the occasion to ask Terman if he didn't think the actor was beautiful.

"I suppose so," Terman said, "though it's not my line."

"Isn't that just the kind of thing a man would say," she said. "I have no difficulty appreciating female beauty—your little friend, Isabelle, for example—without it being quite in my line you know."

He admired her largeness of spirit, he said.

"He's tres jeune, but in important ways mature beyond his years."

"He's been around a long time," Terman said. "I only wondered why you brought him along."

"I'm flaunting him," she said. "Is that what you think? Flaunting or flouting—I'm never quite sure which is the right word." Her leg brushed his or his hers, an accident in which no one admitted being hurt. She said with the cup of tea at her lips, "I'll send him away if you like."

A woman comes into the parlor and offers Henry Berger a cup of tea, which he declines. Beyond the offer of tea, she makes no comment and might have been a servant or the lady of the house with equal plausibility.

When Emile returned she escorted him into another room and Terman, if he made the effort, could hear the murmur of their conversation. It was as though two or three bees had gathered at a closed window to conspire.

Henry Berger sits with his hat in his lap—it is a hat one has rarely seen him wear, a gray stetson from another time. He is waiting for his host to appear.

Emile, who had aged in the intervening minutes, returned to the kitchen to announce the necessity of his departure, some tiresome business with a producer that had slipped his mind. "My pleasure," he said, offering Terman his hand as though it were meant to be kissed. "We will meet again it is my hope."

Terman had seen him in a film at the NFT about three weeks ago—it struck him when the actor said "it is my hope"—an Italian western in which Emile had played one of the two principal villains. He had a breathtaking death scene, somersaulting in air from a blast of gunfire.

The door opens behind him and Henry Berger stands up, turning in no particular hurry to see his friend, Adriano, stride in with outstretched hand, greeting him with an old joke they had once shared. A shadow passes over Henry Berger's face, a mingling of disappointment and disbelief. Perhaps the information he had been given is incorrect or imcomplete and this friend, this partner of his early days, is not the one assigned to terminate his career.

Emile was gone. Marjorie indicated Emile's absence with a wave of her purple scarf as if, by some feat of prestidigitation, she had caused the actor to vanish into air. "The great thing about him," she confided, "is that he is not in the least way possessive."

Emile's disappearance, that well-managed trick, put Terman under a certain obligation to Marjorie, an obligation he had no intention of making known. Each was walking on a cane and Terman thought of them as a matched pair, a remark he heard himself make to his companion, one that pleased him more in consideration than in echo.

They sit facing each other on opposing brown velvet sofas, an octagonal marble table between them. "Is this splendid place yours?" Henry Berger asks him. "Adriano looks around him, assessing his apparent domain. "Would you like a guided tour, old friend? There are more rooms than I ever learned to count." "I'm stunned with admiration," says Henry Berger. "I've had a little luck," says Adriano, motioning to Berger to follow him. "As you probably heard, I retired from the profession a little over three years ago."

"I feel as if I've given up," Terman said, "only there's no one appropriate around to whom I might surrender."

"You poor man," Marjorie said. "If you want to surrender your sword to me, I'll find some use for it."

He took her hand, a transient possession he had no recollection of having acquired, and brought it to his lips. She blushed at the gesture, touched to confusion.

Terman was prey to unobjectified sexual hungers that surged and receded like the tides. An aspect of his fragmentation, he found himself susceptible to Marjorie, whose charms up until the present moment had the weightlessness of myth.

"I find this conversation odd in the extreme," she said.

There is an army of people in the house all pretending not to be there, faces at the windows like faded posters. Henry Berger pretends not to notice the things he sees, follows his old friend through a maze of extraordinary rooms. If the international detective feels his life in some danger, his manner gives no indication of it. More disturbing even than the danger is the apparent treachery of his old friend, who is so ingratiating as he shows him about. Where will he make his move? he wonders. He knows the friend well enough to know that he will not leave the business to a henchman. Adriano leads him out onto a elegant terrace, invites the detective to admire the panoramic view, the mountain stream below, the gray gnarled cliffs which frame the villa on three sides like outer walls. "The vista is most admirable from the south-east," says the friend, leading Henry Berger to a corner of the terrace, stepping back as if to offer him the spectacular vista as a gift. This is where he intends to do it, thinks Berger.

She sat with her legs tucked under her, holding a cigarette she only on rare occasion brought to her lips. Terman came back from the kitchen with a bottle of Muscadet and two champagne glasses. "I like that idea," she said. She rose to her knees, put her arms around his neck and kissed him, the cigarette held behind his head.

The phone was ringing and she called his attention to it but he merely shook his head. "Mightn't it be important?" she asked.

His hand was shaking. "I'd quite like to go into the room with all the mirrors," she said. "That doesn't offend you, I hope. I've always adored that room, though I can see that it might be pall after a while once you've had the initial frisson."

The phone had stopped ringing, but after a few minutes interval began again. "I wish to hell you'd answer it,"she said. He took her cigarette from between her fingers and tossed it into the fireplace. "Don't do that," she whispered. "I don't like things taken out of my hands." The phone was still ringing as they went up the stairs, could be heard now from one of the rooms on the second floor in muffled counterpoint to the ringing downstairs. "Do you know who it is?" she asked him, poking him with her cane. They dueled briefly on the steps, each holding on with one hand to the bannister behind. He knocked her cane from her hand, sent it sprawling over the bannister to the floor below. She gave out a small cry of pain, more shock than pain. The phone stopped then started again. "The room I'm talking about is on the third floor, isn't it?" she said.

This is where he intends to do it, thinks Berger. The old friend is standing a step behind and to the left, has not yet revealed his intention, speaks of the capacity of the landscape to change in different light. "We all change in different light." says the detective. The dark young woman who offered him tea on his entrance, steps out onto the terrace carrying a bowl of olives. Two cars drive up to the other side of the house. "The note I received said you had some information for me," says the detective. "You've been stepping on too many toes," says Adriano. "There are some people in high places that might wish you out of the way." They are facing each other, the hat in Henry Berger's hand held out in front of him. The old friend points to something in the distance while moving his other hand into the pocket of his coat. Henry Berger fires first, his gun under his hat. The impact of the shot sends the friend careening into the side of the villa, his mouth a broken line, eyes frozen open in astonishment. The woman drops the bowl of olives, covers her mouth with her hand. Berger's hat sails over the railing into the ravine below. The detective stands over the fallen Adriano, his gun still drawn. Adriano beckons him with a finger and Berger leans toward him, "One always pays for weakness in the end," Adriano whispers, a gun in his hand pointing at Berger.

The door to the room with the mirrors was closed, a Do Not Disturb notice, the kind used in certain hotels, on the knob of the door, an irrelevancy which nevertheless caused Terman some hesitation. "Is something wrong, luv?" Marjorie asked. He put his ear to the door, listened to heart beat and pulse, the breathing of moths. "Who's in there?" she whispered, leaning over him, the point of a breast pressed to his back like a knife. "What are we supposed to be listening for?" she asked. "This is all terribly amusing."

When he had pushed the door open he was surprised by the fierce unshaven figure coming at him in the mirror. When he turned away for respite the same unenviable figure approached him from another side, and still another.

After she had removed her blouse, mocked on all sides by ghostly imitators, Marjorie said, "It's the kind of bizarre joke my husband would play on one, isn't it? Was that what you had in mind?"

"In this room one gets overwhelmed by self," he said.

Marjorie told a story of how Max had invited some people to a dinner party at their old flat in Knightsbridge and had absented himself before the guests arrived. He had hidden himself somewhere in the diminutive five room flat and the object of the evening was to discover his hiding place. After searching in vain for four or five hours, the guests decided that they were being hoaxed. Marjore had them step out into the hall for five minutes and when she ushered them back Max was waiting for them in the living room. Not only had he been able to avoid discovery, he had also managed to film the search from wherever he was hidden.

"Did they ever get any dinner?" Terman asked.

"You know I don't remember if they did or not," Marjorie said, "though I can't imagine we'd let them go home without any food."

"Perhaps they ate and searched at the same time," he said.

A sudden wind caused the door to the room, which had been ajar, to slam shut.

"I nearly jumped out of my skin," said Marjorie, who had already divested herself of her clothes.

Terman recalled that the door to this room tended to stick, which was one of the reasons the room was rarely used. He could almost remember Max warning him about the door sticking at some inappropriate time in the legendary past.

Marjorie's anecdote had conjured Max's presence.

"It's a bit dazzling, isn't it," she was saying, "seeing yourself like that. One is never absolutely sure if it's oneself or someone else."

Terman kept his eyes closed, spooked by the repetition of images around him, the redundancy of forms. He could imagine the scene being filmed, image within image within image, the camera image no more than a reflection of itself. He wondered if their reflections could fuck while they remained spectators to the event.

"We don't have to do this if you don't want to," Marjorie said. "We could just sit here and talk if you prefer."

Unless the mirrors lied, he was already lodged between her legs. "You're very sexy," he said to her.

"I get off on seeing myself," she whispered. She was articulate to a fault, a scholar of variation, almost every gesture perfectly phrased.

He had a sudden longing to return home, to return to America, that unsceptered continent, to be among people again that spoke the same language.

He had been feigning madness, he thought, or was the pretence itself also madness? Hamlet faced the same dilemma.

Their reflections, he noticed—eyes open for the moment—betrayed more passion, more erotic pleasure, than the supposed originals.

"They expect me to kill you and for that reason I won't," Adriano says. "I won't do their housecleaning for them this time."

"Who's they?" Henry Berger asks.

"I want you to promise me you won't let them hurt Claudia," he says, coughing spasmodically, a trickle of blood at the side of his lips.

"Who gives you your orders, Adriano?"

The dying man's lips quiver at the effort of speech, flutter like boneless fingers. "I promise I'll see to Claudia," Berger says.

Terman lay in bed like a corpse, hands folded across his chest, while Marjorie watched her reflection dress wherever she turned, all sides of her given credence. "You might say something kind," she said.

He wrote himself two lines of dialogue. "You insist on people acting according to some scheme that exists solely in your head. We're all characters in your novel, Marjorie."

"I expect I want to hear that you've had a lovely time," she said.

A third line of dialogue offered itself. "If I said that at your prompting, Marjorie, how could you possible believe it?"

"Trust me, luv."

He perceived himself reaching across the bed to offer some gesture of affection, but in fact he made no such move, made no move at all.

She studied him in the mirror, in the various mirrors, then sat down on the edge of the bed with her back to him. "I think someone must have broken your heart," she said icily.

He roused himself from his torpor. "If Max were a really smart man, he would never leave home," he said.

"It's a start," she said. "Small and incomplete, though not entirely loathsome."

His sleeping prick arose and lifted the covers like the spine of a tent. There was nothing to do for it, no will to accompany its purpose. In a moment or two (perhaps an hour had passed—the man in bed had no sense of time), Marjorie was at the door, negotiating the handle to no effect. He watched her in the opposing mirror.

She cursed the door, kicked at it, promised it the full burden of her wrath.

He planned to get up and help her—there was a trick to the door, you had to push it in to get it out—imagined himself lifting the covers and stepping out of the bed.

She pulled at the handle, turned it both ways, stopped then started again abruptly as if she might deceive the door into releasing her. Terman perceived her as a character in a comic film.

"Bloody bitch of door," she yelled, laughing at herself. She joined him at the bed, the reflections from the four walls of mirrors multiplying her. "Please help me, luv," she said. "The door won't let me out."

Having forgotten their initial combat and its attendant disappointments, he invited her under the covers for a rematch, heard himself speak the words, witnessed the movement of his mouth in one of the mirrors.

"Haven't you had enough of that?" she asked. "Besides, I have to go, I really do. Is that bloody awful of me, darling?"

"Whatever you say," he said.

"It will have to be a quicky-wicky," she said. She removed her off-white pants with the wide cuffs and folded them over the back of a chair, posed for him in the box of mirrors.

When she stripped him of the blanket he shivered from the draft, from a sense of irremediable cold.

The thought struck her, interrupted a separate intention. "It would be just like dear old Max to lock us in," she said. "He has a sense of fun that would make the Marquis de Sade envious."

Max came and went, entered the room and exited without the opening of a door.

Marjorie, surveying the landscape, considered the choices before them. "It'll have to be quick as a wink," she said, reminding them both. She sucked him with lady-like dispatch, a woman of passionate constraints, restored his tower the moment it began to lean. Then she sat on him, facing away, encouraging him to push forward as if he meant to dislodge her. "I always think of it as riding a horse," she said.

She made quick work of him as promised; he was gone before he had so much as arrived. He dreamed someone was in the house, was walking deliberately up the steps, gun in hand. He would have gone to sleep, how easy that was, how right-seeming, but she pulled on his arm until he climbed out of bed. Of course, the door needed opening, required his touch.

"This is the way you do it," he said. He pushed the door in, leaned his shoulder against the frame, then turned the handle down and pulled sharply toward him in one precise infallible gesture.

"It didn't open," she said, laughing nervously. "Is it panic time?"

He tried again without measurable success, embarrassed at his failure. Marjorie walked back and forth from bed to door, generating energy.

"Is someone downstairs?" Marjorie asked, hearing the echo of her own steps.

"It could be Isabelle," he said.

"Will she make a fuss, do you think? I'll say you were showing me the house and the door got stuck." Marjorie threw his clothes at him, worked at straightening the bed. "Don't just stand there," she shouted in a mock-whisper, "Oh, God, I broke a fingernail." Holding the finger to her mouth, sucking on it. A single tear escaped her eye and made its way down her cheek.

Adriano is trying to say something, is marshalling his strength for one last effort. "Trust no one," he mutters. There are footsteps at the door to the terrace and Berger points his gun at the narrow passageway. A gun comes through the terrace door followed by an arm, followed by the figure of a uniformed police officer. "No trouble," says Henry Berger. The old friend in his arms is unconscious, and he puts him down, never for a moment letting the armed policeman out of his sight.

Terman sat at the edge of the bed, picking at a knot in one of his shoelaces, while Marjorie had her ear to the door. From the vantage of the ceiling mirror, they presented a study in angles. "Whoever it is, walks like a cat burglar," she said.

He heard something or thought he did, the exaggerated breathing of someone who had run too fast or was in a state of severe anxiety.

"Will you please get yourself together," she said.

Terman had one shoe on and hefted the other, thought of throwing it at Marjorie.

She caught his eye in the wall mirror and winked. "Whoever it is, I don't believe it's Max," she whispered. "Max has a distinctive step as I should imagine you've noticed."

"I've felt it on my neck,"he said.

"Have you?" she said. "I shouldn't be at all surprised. Mon ami, I really have to be on my way."

The shoelace knot opened in his fingers like a flower. Not all frustrations were without remedy.

"It's not as if I had a choice,"she said. "I really *have* to be somewhere. It's an irreversible commitment."

"I understand that you have to be somewhere," he said.

Terman stood behind her at the door, listening to the news on the other side. The intruder had found his way to the staircase and was coming up the steps.

"Do you have any idea who it is?" she asked. "It's not a housebreaker, is it?"

Imagining that it was his son, Terman declined comment, indicated with a shrug an unlimited set of possibilities.

"Hallo," Marjorie called. "We're locked in a room on the third floor. Could you let us out?"

There was no apparent response and she repeated her request, emboldened to raise her voice so that it seemed to echo through the large house, returning to them like a muted scream. "Please please please," she added.

A door opened and closed below them, a gesture of indifference or contempt. "You say something," Marjorie said to him.

"Who's there?" he yelled in an unused voice. A sudden rage took him. "Damn you," he yelled.

"I hope to god you haven't frightened the person," Marjorie said, banging on the door with her fists. "It's queer, isn't it, that he or she hasn't answered. It wouldn't surprise me in the slightest if Max had sent someone here to murder us both. I should never have mentioned to him that I was coming to your house for tea."

"You mentioned to Max that you were coming here?"

"I wanted to give him back a little of his own," Marjorie said. "I can see now that it was an error of judgment." She tried the door again. "I think I'm getting it, luv. If we both pulled at the same time, don't you think it might make all the difference?"

"We've rounded them all up," says Colonel Lindstrom, putting the gun in his coat pocket as he might a pair of gloves. "All of them except the woman and Adriano." He comes over to check on Adriano's condition, puts his ear to the dead man's chest. "He made you do it, I suppose," he says to Berger.

"I suppose," says Berger.

"Whatever you want to say about his character," Lindstrom says, "he was a man that lived and died by the rules. I suppose he said a few thinks, did he? before he went."

"Only that he regretted dying."

Lindstrom is looking over the railing, his hand in his gun pocket. "Quite a view I should say. What?"

Another man in a uniform comes on to the terrace. "No signs of the woman, sir," he says. "We've taken the place apart with nothing to show for it."

"Keep at it, lad," says Lindstrom. "That attractive young lady is a veritable nest of scorpions. Let's go inside, Berger, before the late afternoon chill gets into the bones."

We cut to the woman, as she's called, letting herself into a crawl space under the lip of the roof.

Marjorie was working on the door, pulling and pushing, making imperceptible progress. "Come over, why don't you, and give us a hand."

Terman went to the window and looked out, saw someone that might have been his son go into the park across the street.

An hour passed and Marjorie wondered out loud whether they oughtn't to break down the door. If they both threw their shoulders into it, she thought, it might do the trick.

"The door is too thick," he said.

"Won't you try even once?" she asked. "You just might be stronger than you think."

To set an example, Marjorie rushed her shoulder into the door and came away in pain. She was looking at the reflection of her martyrdom when she said, "My time spent with you has been the occasion of crippling injuries." For the next few minutes she appeared inconsolable.

Terman thought he heard the outside door open and he mentioned it to her, which eased the pain in her bruised shoulder if only for that moment of illusion.

Henry Berger doesn't like the present business, likes it less and less as it ramifies before him.

"What's your opinion, Henry?" Lindstrom asks him, while his men disassemble the villa. "Are we going about this the wrong way?"

"Why do you want her?" he asks.

"It's the old story, Henry. We want her because she is there."

Berger and Colonel Lindstrom and one of the Colonel's aides, a Chinese sumo wrestler named Yin, go up the stairs to the entrance to the roof, Berger in the advance. Lindstrom says his men have already checked the roof but if Berger wants to take a second look he has no objection. Yin follows him up the ladder to the roof while the Colonel and Sergeant Clark wait below, their guns drawn. Who can tell what Henry Berger is thinking as he walks across the tiled roof, moving methodically from one side to the other, concentrating on the sounds his steps make? "You were right," he shouts down to Lindstrom, stopping at the hollow place where the woman is hiding. "She must have gotten away while you were rounding up the others."

There were moments when Marjorie didn't think about being imprisoned but they had only limited duration. Mostly, she struggled for self-possession. If one didn't panic and went with the flow, she told herself, eventually a way out would present itself. "A situation like this makes one reevaluate one's entire life," she said. "Or do you think that's taking it a bit far?"

Terman looked out the window to avoid being mimicked by his own image, his sense of himself undermined by overstatement. At the last extreme, he could always get the attention of a passerby and ask whoever to notify the police of their entrapment. It hadn't yet reached that moment of urgency. Oddly, in the extended period he had spent at the window, no one had come by on his side of the street.

The urge to account for himself overwhelmed him. "I've been treading water for too long," he said over his shoulder. "Everytime I reevaluate my life, it seems to have fallen off from the year before. I age without getting wiser, tend to forget more than I learn. My relationships with people are as tentative and incomplete as they ever were. More so than ever."

"You need to break with Max," she said, "and go back to your own writing."

"The fact is, I like working with Max," he said. "If I didn't have a screenplay to write, I might sit around drinking beer and staring at the walls. I don't even enjoy going to the movies any more."

"It's not an adult pleasure, is it?" she said. "The first step for you, Terman, is to get away from Max and on to something else."

Marjorie tried the door for what must have been the tenth time, felt it yielding just a little, nothing the eye might acknowledge, but enough to let her entertain a whisper of hope.

Terman had been saying the word "father" to himself. "Father father father father father father father father father father father father father father..." At some point the word evolved from "father" to "farther."

"I felt something," Marjorie said.

He took an andiron from the fireplace and went to the door to see if he could help. The room echoed a sense of contrition.

Henry Berger is standing a few feet away from the downslope of the roof. "You can come out," he says. "Lindstrom and his men have gone."

After a moment or two, a voice comes from the crawl space under the eaves. "I have a gun trained on you," it says. "Throw your gun across the roof and do it quickly. It would please me to kill you."

"I promised your husband I'd keep you from being caught," he says.

"I don't trust you. Throw away your gun."

"Wouldn't I have given you away before if that's what I wanted to do?" When she doesn't answer he says, "I'm going to walk away. If you shoot me it will attract the attention of Lindstrom's men who are sitting in a parked car at the edge of the woods. I'm going now to walk to the ladder at the other side of the roof." Henry Berger turns around and walks slowly toward the other side of the roof.

A trap door opens at the lip of the roof and the woman, not a little crumpled, emerges without attracting Berger's notice. She holds an unusually small handgun and is pointing it at Berger's back when he turns instinctively to face her.

"Will you take me with you?" she asks. "You'll find me a resourceful companion."

They go out the back door of the pensione and move through tall grass towards Berger's car, which is obscured by two large trees. When they reach the car, when Berger unlocks the door to the passenger's side, she presses her handgun to his back. "Take off your jacket and trousers for me, please."

"Are you serious?"

"If you test me," she says, "you'll never know how serious I was."

He undresses without further protest, keeping one hand behind his head as instructed. The widow of his old friend puts his clothes on over her own, while Berger leans against the side of his car with hands behind his head.

"I ought to kill you," she says, "but I don't want to attract attention if I can help it. I want you to open the driver's door with your left hand, keeping the other behind your head. Don't make any moves you'll regret."

"You'll be better off with me than without me," he says. "I'm really quite good at avoiding the police."

"I've already got the better part of your identity," she says. "Take your left hand from behind your head and open the door. When the door is opened, drop the key on the seat, then turn around, take three steps and throw yourself face down on the grass."

"Adriano was lucky to have a woman like you," he says.

"Not lucky enough. Are you opening the door or do I have to shoot you?"

Trying to unlock the car with his left hand, he drops the key to the ground.

"I hate the sight of you," she says. "I despise the way you do things. I hate your preposterous self-satisfaction."

Henry Berger bends down to retrieve the key. As he comes up he turns as if to hand it to her. We see the shadow of his arm moving through the air, followed by the sound of a shot. There is a second shot shortly after the first, then a third.

Dressed again, Berger carries the dying woman back toward the villa.

"I should have killed you the first time I saw you," she says.

"You misjudged my intentions," he says. "I would have helped you get away if you had let me."

"You've done that; I'm away." A thin stream of blood comes from the side of her mouth, keeps coming like a scarf in a magician's trick. "The pain is gone," she whispers. "It just went somewhere else."

Berger puts her down on the grass and sits alongside her, holding her hand. Three cars drive up in short succession. He continues to hold the dead woman's hand, staring into the distance as several men, including Colonel Lindstrom and Sergeant Clark, approach.

They had been trapped in the room for almost five hours and Terman had reached the point where the sight of his own face, no matter the angle of distortion, sickened him. He sat on the bed with his hands over his eyes, besieged by other selves at every turn.

Marjorie had talked non-stop for a time and then, as though her quota of words had run out, had fallen into a protracted silence. Although she heard something, the front door unlocking and someone (a man, she thought) stepping almost noiselessly into the front parlor, she withheld report of the news, superstitious about false alarms.

This time they both heard it, the almost noiseless entry, the hesitant steps in the living room, the uncertain movement of someone who didn't know the house.

"Up here," Terman called out, without turning his head.

"We're locked in a room on the third floor," Marjorie shouted into the door. "Would you let us out?"

"Is it your son?" she asked him.

There was nothing amusing in the situation for Terman, though he discovered a smile on the face of several of his reflections when he allowed himself to turn his head. He had a sense of the same scene playing itself out without resolution again and again. The unknown intruder comes in the house, awakens expectation, then disappears without heeding their cries for help. The incident varied a little on each occasion (the way memory tends to twist events into narrative pattern), though the basic scenario remained faithful to itself.

When she heard someone coming up the stairs Marjorie turned to Terman and winked. The wink recurred in the first two mirrors and then was gone. "In here," Marjorie called. "We're on the top floor." She recovered her cane which was hanging over the back of a chair.

Between calls for help, Marjorie reported the movements of the intruder. After a brief respite on the second landing, he was coming up the stairs to the third floor.

He or she was on the third floor, coming down the long hallway toward them.

"Second door on the right," Terman roused himself to say. He had the premonition that when the door opened, if it ever did, another distorted reflection of his own face would be waiting for him on the other side.

They watched the door handle turn, down and back, down and back, to no startling effect.

Terman took a hand, pulled on the handle as the other pushed against the door. The door remained adamant.

"Put your weight against it," Marjorie advised. "Push with your shoulder."

The mimic in the several reflections mocked all human endeavor.

"It's coming," Marjorie shouted.

The door opened suddenly, severed its restraints, and a man with his own face came into the room.

#

Terman opened his eyes the next morning with a burgeoning sense of self-contempt, regretted the light of day. He had no breakfst, had no need of food, could barely stand to cover himself with clothes. Something was the matter with him or something had been the matter and had cured itself, leaving him untenanted like some derelict building. The air around him, the air he breathed, smelled of neglect.

He dialed Isabelle's number with no expectation of finding her in, so when she answered on the fifth or sixth ring it was almost a dissappointment.

"I didn't expect to find you home," he said.

"I hope that's not why you called. As a matter of fact, I'm waiting for the studio to ring up to find out where I'm supposed to be."

He stammered his request, the question begging refusal. "Why don't we meet for a drink after you finish work?"

"I believe I already have an appointment," she said. "Can't you tell me over the phone what you want?"

He wanted nothing. An unbearable weight of shame oppressed him. "Isabelle, look I'm sorry."

"Yes? That makes two of us, doesn't it?"

"I've behaved unforgivably. I've no excuses."

"I don't want to hear it, Terman. Do you have anything else to say?"

"Isabelle, I'm sorry."

"You don't know what you've done. How can you possibly be sorry?"

"I'm terribly ashamed." He wiped his eyes with the back of his hand, the gesture premature, the tears of shame unrecorded.

"I simply hate this," she said. "If you continue to apologize, I'm going to hang up on you. Don't you have any dignity at all?"

He could do no more than act on the feelings he supposed himself to have. "Could we have dinner tomorrow night?" he asked.

"I don't want to see you," she said in a constricted voice. "Haven't I made that clear? I don't want to see you, not now, not tomorrow, not next week, not next year."

She hung up before he could apologize again, then called back moments later to say she had no business losing her temper at him. "You've done nothing to me I haven't done to myself, have you? I apopogize for hanging up on you, Terman, and for letting you think you had done me some great injustice when you hadn't at all."

He resented her apology, felt it in competition with his own. "You didn't have to call to tell me that," he said.

"I don't know why I called back," she said. "I thought you might come by until I had to leave for work, though I'm not sure that's what I want either. I'm sorry to be so equivocal. It makes me unhappy when you make yourself an abject show and I don't want to subject either of us to that again."

"I can see your point," he said.

"Can you? Terman, what do you want from me?"

"Nothing," he said. He felt himself in a fever of desirelessness.

"Then leave me alone, Terman, will you? Stay away."

"I'll do whatever you want," he said.

"You're not mocking me, are you? Excuse me, someone's at the door." She hung up.

#

There were no transitional moments, no opening and closing of doors. Dressed in a baggy three-piece suit, he was walking south on Abbotsbury Road, the morning unusually warm, the white light of the sun everywhere. He turned left at Leicester Place, walking briskly and without descernible limp. If his ankle hurt him, he avoided the pain by thinking of something else. The white light scorched him. Each step he imagined as the last of its kind, the last he might allow himself within a certain frame of reference. Each gesture supplanted its predecessor, was complete and distinct, never to be recalled or repeated. He walked around the southern end of the park—something he had only done once before—and went along Fillmore Walk to Camden Hill Road. Two burnt-out teen-age girls, lounging in front of a boutique called Sex Sisters, were eyeing him furtively. He turned toward them, nodded, held out empty hands. They put their heads together and giggled. He was struck with the idea of ending his screenplay with Henry Berger walking along a street very much like the one he was on, while a sniper on a rooftop studied him in his sights. The last shot would be of Henry Berger framed (like the subject of a photgraph) in the sights of a telescopic lens. After the picture dissolved to black, *The End* in white on a black screen, we would hear the sound of a gun shot echoing.

Terman went up Camden Hill Road to Holland Street, thought to turn but couldn't without going against himself, made his way to Peele Street where Isabelle had her two room flat. He passed Isabelle's building, went on to the next street, then crossed over and doubled back. He was studying the windows of her aparment when a man working in a garden asked him if he knew the time. He wasn't listening and offered the man a cigarette, which the other accepted with some reluctance. "Ta," said the gardener. "And what's the hour, mate?"

"Eleven o'clock," Terman said without looking at his watch.

"Can't be right," said the other and turned his attention to a wheelbarrow filled with cement.

Giving the time away, Terman felt, was like losing it irretrievably. It was a perception he had had when he was five years old that he had never fully shaken off.

He shadowed her house for hours in his imagination, this shadow of her former lover, accumulating evidence of infidelity and betrayal.

Waiting for Isabelle to answer the door, he could think of nothing to say that would explain the presumption of his visit, trusted to crisis and native wit. He waited five or six minutes—his private clock accurate to a fault—perceiving her continuing absence as further evidence of her contempt. When he knocked the door was opened to him. "You didn't say you were coming over," Isabelle said. "How was I to know?" She was wearing a bathrobe over a slip and looked like she had just taken a bath or been in bed. He embraced her clumsily. "I didn't realize how much I missed you," he said. Her arms circled him without pressure. He was overwhelmed with affection for her, spoke her name with the care one gives a sacred object.

"Did you want to come in?" she asked with a notable absence of conviction. "There's someone else here."

"Someone else and the corpse not yet buried?" He meant it to be amusing, but the words came out etched with bitterness.

"I didn't mean it quite that way," she said.

She preceded him in. The someone, a silver-haired man was sitting in the parlor on a yellow velvet love seat, aggressively smoking a cigar. The men nodded curtly to each other.

Max looked everywhere but at his former collaborator. "I was going to call you as soon as I got to the office," he said. "The news of our project is not so bad, not at all despicable."

Isabelle side-stepped her way into the small kitchen, vanished without explaining herself. "In a moment," Terman said to Max, holding up a finger, and trailed Isabelle into the kitchen, his limp as he followed her insisting on its prerogatives.

"I thought I'd make a pot of coffee," she said, "unless the two of you prefer to have tea." Terman stood behind her and observed his knee brushing the back of her leg. "There's not sufficient room for both of us," she said.

"I want him out of here," he said.

"Tell him that if you like."

Her head bruised his mouth when he kissed her, was backing up as he was coming forward. It struck her as funny but then she apologized for laughing. Terman embraced her from behind, slipped by her, and returned to the sitting room. Max was writing something on the back of an envelope. "Tea about ready?" he asked.

Terman sat in a chair on the other side of the room, turned it so it faced away.

"Would you like a Cuban cigar?" Max asked him. "The real thing."

Terman said, or thought of saying, that there wasn't anything he wanted from Max.

"We're still waiting," Max said, "for the other shoe to fall. Actually there's another project I want to sound you out on. Could you come by the office tomorrow first thing in the morning?"

"I don't think so," he said.

"Prior commitment, is it? Give me a ring at the office and we'll arrange something else, cowboy."

Isabelle returned and sat down at the apex of the imaginary triangle. She had a teapot, three spoons and a bowl of sugar cubes on a tray, but she had forgotten the cups and the pitcher of milk. "I can't go back into the kitchen," she said. "I really can't." She held the tray in her lap, the teapot balanced in the center. Tears overfilled her eyes. "I almost never cry," she said.

"It's true," said Max from behind his cigar. "I've never seen her cry." He rose abruptly from the loveseat as if propelled by this negative recollection. "This is something extremely rare we're privileged to witness."

Terman eased himself from his chair, crossed the room in two strides and, without prior indication of intent, knocked Max down. Max smiled, looked astonished. "I don't understand what's going on," Isabelle said to no one.

Terman took the tray from Isabelle's lap and put it down on an end table. "I'll get cups from the kitchen for you," he said. His thumb hurt and he studied it for signs of dislocation, held it to the light. Max was on his feet, pulling a sweater on over his head, when Terman, without thinking about it, knocked him into the couch.

"There's no need for that," Isabelle said, her head turned away like a partial secret.

Max sprawled on the couch with his fists in front of his face in mock defense. "He has a tendency to overstate," he said. "The next time you hit me, I'll cut your ears off with a razor."

Isabelle came over and put her arms around him from behind. "Be a love," she said, "and go home."

"I haven't finished," he said.

A throw pillow, defining itself in flight, glanced off the side of Terman's head.

Isabelle continued to hold on to him from behind. "I'll come back tonight and stay with you,"she whispered, "if that's what you want."

He said yes and felt the death of desire, the small quenching of a still smaller passion. Only frustration was eased, necessity quieted. He struggled to feel love, to shake and burn with feeling.

His thumb ached. Disappointment arose unbidden, diminished him with its niggardly claim.

"You're the love of my life," he said to her at the door, her hand on his arm, steering him out.

Dismissed, he waited on the street for Max to follow, regretting that he had yielded his place for so small a price. Jealousy passed through him like a sweat of mild fever. In moments Max came through the door, scowling, hair askew from the first kiss of wind, and the former collaborators faced each other as adversaries.

Max pointed a finger at him. "You're lucky I don't bear grudges," The director walked past him then came back, holding a rock the size of his hand. "I'd like to put your face through the other side of your head, you fucking degenerate," Max said.

Terman grinned, though believed himself angry. He held up his walking stick in case the other meant business.

"I'm a civilized man," Max said. "I abhor violence, though when a man abuses me the way you have I'll go to any length to pay him back."

Max backed off when Terman wagged his cane, feinted with the rock which he hefted behind his ear in throwing position.

Their confrontation embarrassed Terman—perhaps worried him too—and he looked for a way out. "An overdose of melodrama," he said, a parody of one of Max's remarks. "I'm sorry I punched you when you weren't looking."

"Apology unacceptable," Max said, though his face relaxed into a self-mocking smile. "If you apologize for the second punch, perhaps we can come to terms."

8

I ran, trying to make it look like a form of exercise and not, what it was, a display of panic. It was not the wisest course of action. I say that from the vantage of retrospection, though I thought at the time I could lose my pursuers. Before I had broken into a run, I had turned a few corners, had doubled back on myself, if only to demonstrate that their continued presence behind me wasn't a coincidence. They were punks, my age or slightly older, parodies of some ideal of ugliness. They had been watching me at Selfridges and may have thought I had taken something to which they had some claim.

I shed them despite their tenacity until I made the mistake of turning up a side street that they happened to be heading down. They were at the far end of the block and may not have noticed me until I turned around and retraced my steps. What else could I have done?

I sprinted this time for about half a mile, and when I got tired I ducked into a crowded bakery and watched them rush by while I waited my turn. The punks were only gone a few minutes before they returned. I could see them in reflection, looking into the windows of shops across the street.

After I left the bakery, getting out I think without being seen, I took refuge in a phone booth and, to justify my act, made some calls.

#

It wasn't so much that I was scared as that I thought I ought to be. I phoned Isabelle and got no answer, then I remembered the old guy that had taken me to lunch and I dialed the first of the two numbers on his card. A supercilious young man (or woman—it was hard to tell) answered and wanted to know my business with Mr. Fitzjohn. "Mr. Fitzjohn asked me to call him," I said, reading the name off the card.

"Yes, but may I ask on what business?" he said with the phony politeness of someone trying to brush you off without giving cause for complaint. "Just tell him the fellow he met at the bookstore is on the phone." I gave him my name. A knock on the glass took me by surprise. A face peered in, mean and witless, the pasty pocked skin like a death mask. It hung there a moment, then disappeared. "Mr. Fitzjohn is in conference," said my informant. "I'll give him the message that you rang up." "He wants to speak to me," I said. "He's been waiting for my call." "Why don't you leave your number with me, Mr. Terman, and I'll have him ring you when he gets out of conference." There was no number to leave and nothing I could say to break through his act. Before I could invent a new story, he had hung up. Holding the dead phone in my hand, I couldn't think why I had called the old guy in the first place. I mean, what could I possibly have expected? Most likely, he would have advised me to call the police. What I wanted was an offer of sanctuary, some place to go where I was safe.

I wasn't without resources. I made a pretend call to the police, shouting into the phone that there were these three punks menacing me. Wherever they were hiding—I couldn't see any of them from the phone box—they were probably too far away to hear my bluff. I was ranting into the phone like some kind of madman, saying whatever came into my head. I couldn't understand why they didn't come at me in the booth. One of them could pull the door open while the other two rushed in and grabbed me. If they charged me, I would have to use the gun to protect myself and I was considering whether it would be enough to show it to them. The idea of teaching them a lesson attracted me, of letting them know they had fucked with the wrong person. I felt a surge of outrage (I was a guest in their country, wasn't I?) and imagined their astonishment when I pointed the gun at them and opened fire. The rat-faced one with the purple hair, the most unpleasant of the three, would fall first, a look of total disbelief on his face, then the tall loose-limbed one with the pocked faced. The fat one, who couldn't keep up with the others, who seemed content merely to hang around with them, would run for his life. And maybe then, I would understand what they were about, would feel their loss like the death of someone close I had wanted to love but hadn't been able to until it no longer mattered. It gave me a lift for the moment, a fast-fading high, to imagine the danger I represented to them.

#

"I have my motor parked just around the corner," Max was saying.

"Why don't we go over to my office, old son, discuss the future of our longstanding collaboration." He dropped the rock he was holding, put an arm around Terman's shoulder and led him to a red Corniche parked illegally just where the street turned on itself.

Although distrustful, Terman offered no resistance, let himself be taken in tow to Max's car. He had no doubt that Max would find some way to exact vengeance when the time was right. The director would not forgive being knocked down, particularly in front of a woman he wanted to impress.

The red Corniche pulled up in front of the Holland Park house.

"This isn't your office, Max," he said.

"It isn't, is it?" said the director who seemed surprised that it wasn't."I just remembered there's someone hanging out at my office I'm trying to avoid. You don't mind, do you? We'll conspire in one of the unused rooms."

Terman pretended he had lost his key or left it behind, went through each of his pockets for Max's witness, feigning distress.

"That was stupid of you," Max said.

"A human error," he said, forgiving Max his crude remark.

"I seem to remember a kitchen window that has a broken lock. Do you know the one I mean?"

"The lock's been repaired," Terman said.

Max studied the situation, removed a key from his wallet. "This just might do the trick," he said.

"A skeleton key?" Terman asked.

Max opened the door. "I have learned, my friend, to be prepared for any emergency that might arise."

In a moment they were inside, shoulders bumping as Max pressed on ahead, moving Terman out of his way. Stationing himself at the kitchen table, Max made seven phone calls to let those who might want to be in touch know where he was staying. After that, they settled in the study, Max behind the desk, Terman on the couch, their habitual configuration.

Max took off his coat, rolled up his sleeves. "To work," he said, withdrawing a script from his briefcase.

"How many nephews does the producer have?" asked Terman, a remark he remembered having made at least once before, and which he promised himself he would never make again.

"Regard," said Max.

It was not, as he expected, another version of *The Folkestone Conspiracies* (AKA "*The Last Days of Civilisation*"), but something else altogether, an unsigned screen treatment of a moderately popular

English novel of two years back. "What am I supposed to do with this?" Terman said. The phone interrupted them, as it would, at approximately eight minute intervals for the next hour. "I want the benefit of a lucid intelligence," Max said.

"Wherever you go," Terman said when Max was free momentarily, "you carry with you the seeds of distraction."

"That doesn't sound quite right," said Max who seemed to be waiting for the next phone call to deliver him from a conversation he had no inclination to continue.

#

I continued moving south, avoiding the mob scenes whenever I could, though also careful not to be caught alone on a side street. I no longer made any effort to get away from them, pretended indifference to their pursuit. They kept out of sight much of the time so when one or another appeared, popping out of some storefront as I passed, it was always a shock.

#

Max was lordly on the phone, threatened, cajoled, dispensed rewards, talked in voices Terman had never heard him use before. On one occasion he seemed to be offering the Holland Park house for someone else's use. "What's going on?" Terman asked.

"This doesn't concern you, cowboy," said Max. "Not to worry. I'm going to take a bath and change my shirt if it's all the same to you. You might use the time to review the script I showed you." He sailed the thick envelope at the couch, Terman ducking under it as it approached his head. "If anyone rings up while I'm in the bath, would you take the number down and say Mr. Kirstner will ring back in a bit. I'd appreciate it if you could do that."

"Is the Henry Berger project dead?" he asked.

"Chancy," Max said. "Hanging on."

"Are we going into production?"

"Max made a gesture with his hand that indicated the remotest of possibilities. "Some of the money we expected has dried up. The script has got too many private jokes that only you and I understand. Do you get what I'm saying?"

When the phone rang Max asked Terman if he would answer it and take the caller's number.

If that was all that Max wanted, it was easily enough done, yet he held back, letting the contemplation of a response suffice for the response itself.

"What are you waiting for?" Max asked.

"I'm waiting for the other shoe to drop," said Terman. "I'm waiting for all the money to be in place."

Max yawned, turned his back to him. "If you don't want to work with me on this project," he said, "you're perfectly free to go your own way."

The moment Terman lifted the phone to say hello, it had silenced.

"It doesn't matter," Max said, his abruptness belying the remark. He left to take a bath like a man leaving on a flight into space.

#

Terman stepped out into the hall and listened to the sounds of Max wallowing in his bath. When it was quiet he imagined that Max had fallen asleep in the tub, that leonine head slipping by degrees into the steamy water. The melodrama of Max drowning in his own bath gave him a certain satisfaction like a bad film that fulfills the crude expectations it has itself set in motion. He knocked on the door of the bathroom. "Find your own," Max said. "This one's mine."

What else might happen? The ringing of the phone recalled him to his study. "Dad," the voice said, "I'm glad I reached you. I'm having some kind of trouble with these three guys."

"Where are you?"

"Broadwick Street, I think. It's about a mile southwest of Oxford Street." He had difficulty catching his breath.

"I'll come for you in the car," he said, though once made, he regretted the offer, felt exploited.

"You don't have to if you're busy," Tom said. "It may not be anything at all. These three punks—they're just kids really—have been following me for over an hour. I don't know what they want and I don't think I want to find out. They're rather horrendous looking actually." He laughed his nervous laugh.

"Why don't you call the police?"

"I can't do that. I think you understand what I'm saying."

Terman couldn't admit that he didn't. "I'll come down in the car and get you. At this time of day, it'll take at least twenty minutes."

"I didn't mean for you to come after me. I mean, that wasn't the reason I called."

"You don't want me to come or you do?"

"The phone booth I'm in is in front of a pub called The Wycherly Arms. There's a Pizza Land and a Sketchley's down the street on the same side and a Chinese Restauant with these skinned ducks hanging in the window across the street. If you don't see me, I'll be moving around. Look for me in front of the pub or in the phone box. Okay?"

"I'll be there as soon as I can, Tom. Don't take any unnecessary risks."

"So in about twenty minutes, right? I'm depending on it."

#

What he felt before, what he had named as rage, was nothing to the bloodstorm in his head as he unlocked the door of the car, as he climbed in behind the wheel, as he fought the key into the ignition. What he didn't know was whether his anger was directed at Tom for getting into trouble or at the thugs harassing him.

He was off, debating the unmoving traffic, rushing and stopping to no useful purpose, unforeseen obstructions at every turn. Attempting to circumvent the worst of the traffic, he took himself further and further out of the way, wanting above all to keep moving. The trip would take longer than estimated, perhaps twice as long, and he could imagine Tom thinking that he wasn't coming or that he had intentionally delayed. He found his son's distrust unforgivable.

Terman drove down Holland Park Avenue, which turned into Notting Hill Gate, then turned south on Kensington Church but the traffic was so dense it seemed preferable to make his way on narrow side streets. Each new route seemed less felicitous than its predecessor and so he rued his choices, his judgment awry. The more frustrated he became the more he resented his errand. He could readily imagine Tom, accosted in the phone box by the toughs, pulling out his father's revolver in a moment of desperation. What would follow? If the gun were loaded, and if there were no other choice, Tom might wound one of the boys to frighten them away. More than likely nothing exceptional would happen. It was not impossible that Tom had made up the story about being followed or had exaggerated an ordinary street confrontation into melodrama. It was melodrama, however, that teased Terman's imagination, the pleasures of the improbable.

#

I watched them huddle together in front of a record shop, looking over toward me as they conspired. They wanted trouble, were addicted to it, and they had fixed on me as their target. So I knew when they walked off that it was only a ruse and that they would be back, hoping to catch me off-guard. What I didn't expect was that they would show up again as quickly as they did. One of them, the one with the purple streaks in his hair, showed his head from around the corner opposite the street they had turned up. When he saw that I was watching him he scuttled back. They had concocted some cretinous plan, had split up and were laying for me, supposedly out of sight, in three different spots. A dessicated woman, about my mother's age, who had been standing outside the booth, knocked on the glass with a key. I opened the door without thinking. "Do you mind, luv?" she said, squeezing past me.

#

It was hot in the car, his shirt sticking to his back, and he unrolled the window while waiting for the light to change. The light defied anticipation, stayed red for a prolonged time. Terman took the occasion to open the street guide on the seat next to him, to check again where he had to go. The light was still red when he looked up and he thought just my luck to get stopped indefinitely at a broken light. A horn honked from behind, a mild squawk. Even after three years in England, he tended not to understand, or pretended not to, the mysteries of London traffic. He drove like an American, he thought, justifying his negligence.

The light was still red. He remembered, or had the illusion of remembering, the day he announced to Kate and Tom that he was moving away. He had put it off as long as he could, awaiting a moment when such unsettling news might be given with grace and reassurance. It was when he recognized that no such moment would ever arrive, that there never had been and never would be an appropriate moment to tell his children he was leaving them, that he was able to tell them at all. Kate, who was seven and a half, went to her room and closed the door, saying she didn't think she wanted to talk about it now. He remembered her marching out of the living room like an adult, like the person she might imagine herself becoming fifteen years later. He called after her to say he would visit on weekends, that it wasn't as if he were leaving forever. "Don't lie to her," Magda said. "Once he steps out that door we'll never see him again." Tom, who was four, for whom none of it made much sense, was sitting on his lap. "Would you read me a book?" he asked. Terman said he would but first he wanted to see if Kate was all right. "It's not fair," Tom said. (Even then, particularly when his own wants were at issue, he had a passion for invoking justice.) Terman said, "You pick out a book and I'll come right back and read it to you." When he came into Kate's room she was lying on her bed, facing the wall. She was stoney, had willed herself into an inanimate state. "It'll be all right, Kate," he said in a weary voice. "I promise you." He put his hand on her shoulder, tried to turn her toward him. She was so rigid there was no moving her without the use of force. She was still immobile when he gave up and left the room. Perhaps if he had stayed with her, it would have made a difference in both their lives. In the living room, on the yellow corduroy couch, Magda was reading to Tom from *The Wizard of Oz*. He offered to take over but Magda said nothing doing. "We'd like you to go," she said. He stood his ground, thwarted. "See you soon, Tom," he said. There was no answer or none he remembered, neither wave nor nod. "Read," he said to his mother and Magda repeated in an overly inflected voice the sentence she had read when he entered the room.

The light was still red. He was thinking it was odd how rarely he went to the movies in London during the past year. Once a month on the average and more often than not to the National Film Theater or the ICA. It was particularly odd because he used to go all the time, an insatiable witness, addicted to images in the dark, finding miraculous accidents in the most commonplace work. The light was green (finally), but the cross street was backed up and the light came red again before he could move through. Terman turned the car around and went the other way, took a left and then another left. A woman he thought he knew—it was odd how familiar and unfamiliar she was at the same time—was walking on the right side of the street, rapt in self-absorption. He rolled down the passenger window and called her by the first name that came to mind.

#

Before I could think of anything to say—I have trouble getting my story together—she was in and I was out. In a panic I stood with my back to the phone box for the longest time, waiting for her to finish her call. After a point, I walked over to Pizzaland. One of the punks, the smallest of the three, a ferret-faced kid with acne scars, emerged from the doorway. He grabbed my arm but I was too strong for him and knocked his hand away. When he brought out a penknife I had no choice but to show him the gun and, in a gesture I regretted even before its conclusion hit him with it across the face in an awkward jabbing motion. Then I ran in what I thought to be the only safe direction available. I didn't look back, though I assumed the other two, if not all three, were converging on me. I don't know what I regretted most, that I had hit him with the gun or that I hadn't hit him hard enough. If I could keep away another ten minutes, I estimated, my father would appear with the car. Then I had the perception—it came unbidden which gave it added weight—that my father had seemed unsurprised at my news. I mean, why shouldn't it surprise him that these three punks were trailing me around London. What did he know that I didn't? Whatever his part in the business—I didn't actually believe he had hired these kids to harrass me—I began to have doubts that he would show up as promised. He was capable, I knew, of finding excuses for indefinite delay. I didn't see my pursuers when I glanced over my shoulder, but then one of them turned the corner and pointed a finger at me.

#

"My name isn't Isabelle," the woman said in an American accent.

The woman looked more like Magda than Isabelle and perhaps thinking of Magda, he had confused the two. "Excuse me," he said.

When he stopped at the next corner for a light she wandered over to the car. "What a series of coincidences," she said. "First at the airport and then here. Don't tell me you still don't know me."

"Why should it matter whether I know you?"

"It matters to me. It makes me distrust my own identity if someone ignores me. Where are you going, Terman? Maybe you can drop me off somewhere on the way."

The light had changed and the car behind him registered mute disapproval. "I'm going to Broadwick Street," he said. "Do you know where Broadwick Street is?"

She came around the other side and climbed into the passenger seat, transferring the street guide to her lap. "I haven't the smallest notion," she said. "What's there?"

She deigned to read the street guide for him while Terman rushed obliquely to his destination, detouring whenever traffic blocked his way.

"You were so awful to me at the airport," she said. "I don't know why I'm doing you a favor. I didn't even like you much in the old days when we were all such good friends."

Terman had to jam on the brakes to keep from hitting the car that had stopped abruptly in front of him. He held out his arm to keep Lila from pitching forward.

"I'm surprised you didn't let me hit my head," she said. "I used to think—it was also Magda's opinion—that you were the most self-centered person of our acquaintance. Still, you were nice with the children at times, you really were. Take a left at the next corner. Was it that you didn't like adults or that you didn't like me and my then husband, or was it that you were secretly shy? I always meant to ask you but in those days I didn't have the courage. It's different meeting someone years later in another country. You always looked so angry, you know, so fierce really as if you wanted to kill anyone who got in your way. I thought of you, you'll laugh at this, as a buccaneer. It was undeniably attractive in a certain way, though I think one had to have a masochistic streak to find it so. Take a left here. Tell me the truth. What was your impression of me in those days?"

He edged his way through traffic, trailed by some unnamable dread. That it mattered to him that he reach Tom was indication that he was capable of feeling. His sense of urgency was in itself like passion. He sensed, on the other hand, that he would probably never reach Tom and that in the long run it wouldn't matter. Before he knew it, he was there. He drove down Broadwick at ten miles an hour, waiting for Tom to declare himself. A trick had been played on him. There was no Sketchley's, no Chinese restaurant with ducks in the window, no phone in front of a pub called Wycherly Arms. "Could there be another Broadwick Street?" he asked her.

"Oh my," she said. "Will you ever forgive me? We're on Broadwick Place not Broadwick Street." She checked the street guide, advised him to take a right turn at the corner they had already passed.

He swung the car around, an ill-timed audacity, a taxi coming the other way. He lived through the collision—the black Austin smashing into their left side as they turned—before he realized the cab had managed an abrupt stop inches short of contact.

The driver shouted at him, "Trying to get us all killed, are you?"

Terman had nothing to say in his defense, drove on with his head down, turning left at the appropriate street.

"You should have apologized to him," Lila said.

"What difference would it have made?"

"You're as incorrigible as ever, aren't you? I don't know why I allowed myself to get into this car."

The phone box in front of The Wycherly Arms was unoccupied when he drove past, Terman discovering the pub only as it receded before him. He pulled up to the curb at first opportunity, kept the motor running. Tom's absence determined the landscape.

"I'll get out and take a bus," she said. "I don't want to get in the way."

Two of the punks appeared on the other side of the street, shrunken and demented figures, sexually ambiguous, arms around each other's shoulders like lovers. One of them might have been a woman, though it was impossible to tell which one. They seemed to him more pathetic than dangerous. He sat hunkered down in the car, observing them.

"I don't know when I've had so much excitement," Lila said.

Terman got out of the car after a few minutes and walked to the front of the pub. He peered into the back garden where a young couple sat eating what looked like bangers and mash, a child with a stuffed fox in its lap asleep in a stroller behind them. The commonplace scene fascinated him and he forgot for the moment the object of his search, or imagined himself as the object, the lost and forgotten child. The couple spoke German and he wondered at their apparent ease in this foreign place.

The sight of his son coming toward him took away his breath, made his chest ache, brought tears to his eyes.

Tom had his head down, barely acknowledged his father as he came up to him. They walked together to the car and Tom got in back slamming the door after him.

As they drove quickly away, Terman glimpsed the two punks staring at them, one had his fist raised threateningly,the other (the woman?) made a face like a gargoyle.

They escaped the street, rushing away in silence like thieves. "Do you remember me?" Lila asked, smiling at Tom. "My husband, Stanislaus and I used to be neighbors of yours. You used to play with my son Petey, when you were both much younger."

Tom nodded.

"Are you all right?" Terman asked him.

"I'm on my last legs," Tom said, laughing nervously. He held out his hands. "No stigmata yet. I had a few bad moments right before you came. And I thought for a while, you know, because you took so long, that you weren't coming."

"Did you ever find out what those boys wanted from you, Tom?" Lila asked.

Tom mumbled something unintelligible, then said, "They were up to no good."

"I didn't get that," she said. "Perhaps you didn't want me to get it.

I'm going back to America tomorrow and I thought I'd tell your mother that I saw you and that you were in one piece. You are in one piece, I hope."

"The only injuries are internal," he said, playing to her as if she were an audience in a theater. "What you see is what you get."

"Where do you want to be dropped?" Terman asked Lila, though Tom thought the question was meant for him and said it didn't matter.

"You can drop me at a bus stop," Lila said. "What's your destination?" They had been driving in circles.

"I'll take you wherever you want to go," he said. "I don't want you reporting to Magda that I mistreated you." He meant it as joke, or thought he did, though he could see from the flicker of perception on Lila's face that she believed he was dependent on Magda's opinion of him. Whatever Lila might say in his favor, Magda would be unimpressed. "He went out of his way for you," she would say to Lila, "because he wanted Tom to think better of him."

After a while, he found himself alone with his son.

#

Even though we were packing to leave, I was embarrassed for the room, wanted it to show itself to better advantage. Some pink roses Astrid had given me had withered away in their plastic vase, though the dead flowers were better than none at all, I thought, gave off the memory of flowers. As mediocre as the room was, I wanted him to admire it, to perceive in it endearing qualities that I had somehow missed. It was a room I had lived in and now would no longer live in.

"I'd like you to return the things you've taken," he said, glancing away from the ill-gotten goods I had laid out on the bed.

"I can't bring them back without asking for trouble," I said. "Most of it's not worth anything anyway."

"That's not the point."

"Well," I said. "I mean, what is the point as you see it?"

"You won't do it again?"

It was easier to say I wouldn't than to say I wasn't sure so I told him what he wanted to hear. Anyway, I never thought of it as going on forever; each theft seemed final in itself.

We heard the door to Mrs. Chepstow's apartment close softly, the click like a sound made with one's tongue.

"Give it up," he said, staring out of the room's only window.

"Give up what?"

"You don't want to have to come back here again," he said. "It's cleaner to move everything out, make a final break."

Cleanliness had never excited me much, nor had final breaks. I mentioned that I owed the landlady some money and he said he would take care of it, whch wasn't what I had in mind.

"She doesn't really care about the money," I said. "She likes to have me in the house."

He sat down in my one chair (I still thought of it as my chair) and stared ahead of him in disapproval. "What if I lent you the money and you paid her," he said. "Would that make it all right?"

"I don't like to rush into anything," I said.

He looked sick, so I said if he wanted to pay her, if that would gratify him, to go ahead.

I picked up the valise to carry down the stairs and my father said he would take it and pulled it from me, then I tried to take it back. "I can handle it," I said.

We were both holding on to it, then both let go, the overstuffed valise falling to the floor with a thud. He apologized for letting it drop and I said well it was my fault too, then I remembered something and reached under the bed for a copy of a book I had stashed there.

"Is there more?" he asked, dragging the valise to the door.

"I thought you might be interested in having this," I said, my voice full of phony self-amusement. I handed him the novel which was not in the best condition, having been scrunched in my jacket among other displaced possessions.

"I've been looking for copies of this," he said, clearly upset at its condition. "I'm very pleased to have it, Tom." He came over as if to put an arm on my shoulder then stopped himself, or else had never intended any more than an undefined step toward me. "Where did you come on it?" he asked.

"It came on me," I said or something equally ambiguous. I imagined he thought I had taken it from his study and was now giving it back under the pretense of a gift. There were a few other things under the bed I had somehow forgotten and I thought it might be a mistake to leave them behind for Mrs. Chepstow to take to heart. I filled my jacket pockets with odds and ends.

He was still unbending the book, worrying it back to its origingal condition. "This novel was rejected twenty-seven or twenty-eight times in America over a four year period before it found a publisher," he said. "If for that reason alone, it's been my favorite. I reworked it a number of times, trying to make its obvious flaws less apparent. I doubt that I made it any better but when it appeared in print what had been wrong with it miraculously vanished."

"Well, I'm glad I got the right book," I said, "the appropriate symbol."

I carried the valise down the stairs, my father occupied with his book. He stopped at the landlady's apartment and knocked forcefully at the door, demonstrating how to make his presence felt.

It was odd that she didn't answer right away; she tended to live close to the sound of things, eager for some invasion of her lonely privacy.

"She must be taking a nap," I said.

I tried the door and discovered it unlocked, and we looked at each other with what I thought to be some kind of understanding.

"I'll leave a check for her on the table in the hall," he said.

#

Terman called, "Hello," opening the door just enough to permit his voice to carry, thought he heard something in reply, a hiss, a muffled groan. He called again, heard what sounded like the echo of his own voice.

"Let's go," Tom said. He picked up his suitcase and they walked down the remaining flight of steps to the front door. Terman heard something from upstairs that turned him around, an ashtray falling or the slamming of a window, the whispering of conspirators, the creak of steps. He wrote a check for sixty pounds and left it on the long table in the foyer, considered his obligation discharged.

The car was unusually sluggish, moved as if it were riding through sand, which seemed perfectly reasonable to the driver, an extension of some feeling about himself. It was Tom who suggested that something might be wrong. He got out and discovered that a back tire was flat. The slash marks just above the tread indicated sabotage.

Tom got out of the car and offered his regrets. Father and son stood bent over the damaged tire in shared grievance.

Why only one tire? Terman was wondering. It seemed, if nothing else, a failure of the imagination.

#

Henry Berger enters the almost pitch-black interior of an abandoned church, whistling to himself. As soon as he adjusts his sights to the dark, he determines a figure standing next to the pulpit.

"Don't come any closer," a voice says,a burnt out whisper. "I am of no use to you once you know who I am. Please turn your head."

(The figure in the shadows is tall and angular, elongated even further by the shadows.)

"I understand you have some information for me." Henry Berger says.

"I have no information for you," says the other. "I can tell you nothing. If you're going to discover you've been moving in the wrong direction, you'll have to do it on your own power."

"And how do I do that?"

"It's your view, I understand, that as eight figures on a certain list of ten have died in suspicious circumstances, one of the two remaining figures is the assassin?"

"How do you know what my view is?" Berger turns himself slightly to the left, inclining his neck.

"I've asked you not to move," says the voice. "Your pursuit of this assassin has occasioned, what?, five additional murders, the killing of accomplices, the covering over of tracks."

"Who am I talking to?"

"A whisper in the dark, a disembodied voice. The real assassin is above suspicion, long since discarded from your concern."

"Are you telling me that the murderer is not a member of the so-called Folkestone Conspiracy?"

"You persist in misunderstanding me," says the voice. "I've not said that everyone on that list is above suspicion. In your pursuit of the simple, Mr. Berger, sometimes you overlook the brillantly complex. I have only a few more minutes to spare. Do you understand what it is you don't know?"

Berger is silent, takes a deep breath. "The assassin is on the list of ten, but is not one of two presumably still alive. You're indicating that the murderer is one of the murdered. One of the apparently murdered. Is that right?"

"That's at least one of the possibilities," says the sandpaper voice. "The pursuit of this assassin may take you places you had been better advised to avoid. Mr. Berger, please count off ten seconds to yourself before going through the main doors. I suggest this measure for our mutual security."

Berger counts slowly to five, then stops abruptly. "Why are you telling me this?" he asks. "How do I know I can trust you?"

Henry Berger turns abruptly in the direction of his informant, his gun in hand. For as far as the eye can see, there is nothing.

#

Terman unlocked the door to his house, handed in Tom's suitcase, was about to close the door when he noticed someone sitting on the sofa, head tilted forward.

"Is that you, Max?"

The figure seemed to move his head forward in approximation of a nod.

"What are you doing?" Terman asked.

"I'm thinking," the figure said in a midwestern accent. "Does that meet with your approval?"

"Are you a friend of Max Kirstner's?"

The weary nod was repeated, a gesture so small as to deny its moment as it passed.

This odd presence disconcerted him. "Is Max in the house somewhere?"

The figure seemed to shrug, though it may only have been the effect of the damp chill in the room. "Are you through asking questions?" he asked. "I don't like being interrupted when I'm worrying an idea. So if you don't mind."

When he got back to the taxi in which Tom was waiting, he instructed the driver to take them to the Tate Gallery. He made no mention of the intruder in his living room.

"To tell you the truth," Tom said, "I'd rather do something else."

"We'll go wherever you like," Terman said.

"The thing is, I don't know where I want to go, Dad. Could you suggest some places?"

It felt to him as if his skin were being cut away in narrow strips. He recited a litany of names. "The Tower of London, The National Gallery, The British Museum, St. Paul's Cathedral, The Houses of Parliament, Westminster Abbey."

"I have difficulty looking at things," Tom said, his tone apologetic. "No powers of concentration."

They arrived in front of the Tate without having decided on a destination.

Terman paid the driver, the bill coming to a pound forty more than recorded on the meter, one of the mysteries of London travel he had never resolved. Nothing ever cost what it appeared to cost.

Instead of going into the museum, they crossed the street and walked along the bank of the Thames toward Westminster, the direction as arbitrary as the walk itself. After a point they sat on a bench facing the river, though for all the attention they paid it, they might have had their backs to the water. Terman was thinking how the disappointments they felt in each other's company seemed to multiply, seemed to carry the weight of earlier disappointments, seemed to carry the weight of disappointments between fathers and sons impressed in the history of the race. Tom took off his workboots and socks and massaged his feet. "I'm cold," he said.

Terman took off his jacket—he himself was sweating from the heaviness of the weather—and handed it to Tom. The boy put it on over his field jacket, struggling to get his arms through the sleeves. It didn't work and then it did. No matter what he did, he couldn't get the buttons to close.

"Just wear it over your shoulders," Terman said.

Tom shook his head—that it didn't fit was another disappointment—and he returned the corduroy jacket to his father who was disappointed to have it back. "When I'm cold," he said, "it doesn't matter how much I wear. Sometimes I walk around the house with four or five layers of clothing on and I can't get warm."

"That sounds terrible."

"It's not so bad," Tom said. He hugged himself, stood up, sat down, blew into his hands which he then rubbed together. "There are worse things," he said, "aren't there? I mean, people are starving in Cambodia."

His father's shadow seemed everywhere in evidence, seemed to grow more oppressive even as its source diminished. Tom felt deprived of language in the presence of that shadow, aware of the self-consciousness of his least remark. The more he faulted himself, the more he blamed the other for being the occasion of his failure.

"Let's walk some more," Terman said.

They walked along the bank to Westminster Bridge then crossed over to the other side of the Thames. Tom was cold, still cold.

They stopped for something to eat in a cafeteria in the basement of Royal Festival Hall, though in fact neither ate. Tom wanted nothing. Terman, though hungry—the same unappeasable hunger he had felt all week—abstained. He had a cup of black coffee, the fluid thick as ashes.

Terman imagined their time together as a segment of a film. You could perceive them from overhead, from one side (or the other) from front or back, in close-up or medium shot, or through metaphoric correlative. The father was smoking a cigar; the son sucked idly on a drinking straw, the accompanying can of Coca Cola of no interest to him. The pained looks on their faces might be mirror images of one another, though otherwise the resemblance was slight, almost circumstantial. They had learned to look like one another, had grown that way.

Purposelessness, thought Terman. What wasn't? He damned the waste of time and even so the aging process increased its pace, denied escape, denied intention.

They were either at each other's throats or stiff and formal, a pair of wire coat hangers in the same closet. "I live by my wits," Tom wanted to say, "so have more trouble surviving than most." His tongue was tied. He couldn't take anything from his father, not even a can of Coca Cola, without feeling like a sellout, disloyal to his mother, a thief of self.

Terman was aware as they sat dawdling over cold coffee and warm Coca Cola that time was passing at some accelerated rate, that there were jobs of work he had set himself to do not being done. Years back, before he had given himself to screenwriting, he had outlined a series of ambitious novels that would take him the rest of his life, or longer, to complete. He had started the first, had put it aside to work on the second, and had discarded both at some point to earn his keep. What he had done (more than a thousand pages in manuscript), what he had set himself to do, barely interested him any longer. Only the sense of urgency remained.

"What should we do now?" he asked his son.

9

If I were the central figure of my own narrative, I might have conceived some final reckoning with the three punks. It would have been a different story: gunfire, spilled blood, violent deaths, an end once and for all to the claims of rebellion. They might even kill my father, stab him with a knife or beat him over the head with a tire iron. It would make my position clearer, give me traditional cause for vengeance. The one with the purple streaks in his hair might hold a gun to my head and fire an empty chamber. When I survive it's as if I've already lived one life and gone into another. I would roll over on to my side, pull out my father's gun, come up firing. The gun makes a final statement, as they say, has the last word.

The punks have been hired by Max Kirstner, who wants the writer, L. Terman, out of his way.

Or they have been hired by Terman, at Max Kirstner's advice, and have taken matters into their own hands, have double-crossed their employer.

The final episode would be between Max and Tom on one of the balconies at St. Paul's Catherdral. Max would try to push Tom off but Tom would step aside, and Max, propelled by his own thrust, would fall headlong to his death.

Sometimes the teller of the story has few prerogatives of his own, is carried along by (the logic of) events. In real life, heroism is just getting through the day.

My father is in a phone box, attempting connection with the outside world. As I can't hear him, I can only imagine his conversation. I imagine the phone ringing without respite. My father, thinking he has dialed the wrong number, hangs up, rests his head against the side of the booth. He thinks: each gesture is more pointless than the last. Or rather I am thinking it for him, imagine the language passing through his consciousness like rats in the stays of a canal. (He's not so bad when you get to know him.) He will dial again holding the two pence piece in his other hand, holding it between thumb and forefinger of that hand. There is an answer this time and the coin is inserted in the slot. A voice appears.

#

Terman felt a spasm in the muscle of his left arm, a dull spasmodic pain from elbow to shoulder. He flexed his arm a few times, massaged his shoulder, trying not to call attention to his concern. If he were dying, if his heart were failing him, he intended nevertheless to finish out the day.

"What are we going to do when we leave here?" Tom asked.

"We could go to a movie if that interests you."

"Yeah, I'd like that ," Tom said.

They walked over to the National Film Theater—they had been heading toward it all along—to see if there was anything worth seeing. It had been Terman's recollection that *The Conversation* was playing, though he turned out to be mistaken. At the NFT 2, there was a 4:00 showing of something called *Bright Eyes*, part of a series on child stars, and at the NFT 1 (at 4:15) was Brian De Palma's *Obsession* which he had seen twice before.

Tom said *Obsession* interested him but he didn't want to press his father to see something he had already seen. Terman said he was curious to see how well it stood up. They got on the end of a queue that extended outside the door and wound, two and three deep, around the side of the building.

Tom said he thought the English couldn't live without queues, that they lined up in their own homes to go to the bathroom, his voice carrying, attracting a few stares.

Terman felt the time pass as they inched forward in the disorderly queue, felt that his life would be almost over by the time they reached the window at which the leftover tickets were being sold.

"I have two together in Row A," said the icy young woman behind the glass, "and a single in Row B. Those are the last three I have."

"I'll take the two in Row A," Terman said, taking a five pound note from his wallet.

"May I see your card?" she said.

He knew his card had been missing for weeks and he made the

obligatory show of searching for it in his wallet. "I can't seem to find it," he said, "but I promise you I have one."

The young woman, who wore large tinted glasses, seemed impervious to human appeal, said you're supposed to show your membership card when you purchase tickets.

Tom produced a dog-eared card, palming it so his father couldn't read the name on it, and the tickets were issued.

"I didn't know you had a membership," Terman said. Tom shrugged, started to explain, ended up nodding his head.

The auditorium was already dark when they reached their seats, which were in the far left-hand corner of the first row. The movie was starting, had started, flickering images above them and to the right. An elegant, dreamlike party ends in a bizarre kidnapping. The wife and small daughter of the wealthy and sympathetic (and complacent) protagonist are held for ransom. The police are brought in, mishandle their pursuit. The kidnappers' car runs into a gas truck and explodes. The wife and daughter are apparently killed.

It was hard to see things clearly when you were sitting right under the screen. Tom was breathing noisily as if in a crisis of anxiety. Years pass and the hero, still grieving the loss of his wife, vacations in Italy where he meets an art student who bears an extraordinary resemblance (they are both played by the same actress) to the woman he mourns. He falls for this ghostly double of his former wife, believing (at some level, one suspects) that it is the dead wife herself miraculously restored. The obsession is with restoration, with the illusion of immortality.

Tom took something out of his jacket and held it guardedly in his lap, both hands over the undefined object.

The girl has a history distinct from his own and is much too young to be the lost wife. No matter her apparent history, the resemblance is irresistible. He proposes to bring this youthful incarnation of his dead wife back to America and marry her. If he distrusts his own motives—this fixation with an image a kind of madness—he must also believe that their circumstantial meeting, like his wife's circumstantial death, is an aspect of divine providence. Taken away arbitrarily, the woman he loves is mysteriously returned to him. Not the woman, but the image of the woman. Something is wrong, which it serves him to ignore.

His eyes on the screen, Tom transferred whatever he had in his hands to his father's lap. It had the weight of a heavy stone, and Terman's first conflicted impression was that Tom meant him some harm by it. His unpursued impulse was to stand up and let it fall to the floor. A glance was sufficient to identify the object as a revolver similar to the one taken from the desk in his study, and he put his program notes over it to keep it out of sight.

Using his left hand, he moved the gun (sandwiched inside the program notes) from his lap to the side pocket of his corduroy jacket.

When he looked up again at the screen his eyes burned from the proximity of the image. The presence of the gun in his pocket, its unexplained return, distracted him from the illusory action of the movie, an action that tended, despite his familiarity with it, to take him by surprise.

The mystery resolves itself through flashback. The woman who resembles the hero's wife turns out to be his lost, presumed dead daughter. (The exposition seemed beside the point, the demystifying of a dream.) There is the reprise of a dance at the end, father and daughter whirling around and around.

When they were outside Tom said, "It was fantastic. *Very* strange." The experience of the movie seemed to exhilarate him. "It doesn't really make sense, does it?"

Terman didn't like to talk about films immediately afterward, liked to be haunted by them for as long as possible. "It makes its own sense," he said to no one.

They walked across a footbridge to the Charing Cross tube stop and took the Bakerloo to Oxford Circus where they changed for the Central Line. In transit between stops, Terman had the premonition that the train would never arrive at its next destination, that the shadow zone between stations was the real world stripped of illusion.

When they came up from the underground at the Holland Park station, Tom said he was hungry. Terman said that the moment Isabelle got back they would go out to a neighborhood Indian restaurant that wasn't half bad, then he remembered that Isabelle was not expected to return. He was suddenly aware of the weight of the gun in his pocket and he put his hand on it to verify its presence.

"Did it stand up on reseeing?" Tom asked.

"There are some things I can't get enough of," said Terman.

#

On one of their daily outings, Tom broached the subject of Isabelle's absence. "It ran its course," Terman said. And another time: "We're on temporary vacation from each other."

From time to time Terman called Max to ask when the man upstairs might be expected to leave. He was told that there was no available hotel space in London during August, but that they (undefined) were trying to work out a solution acceptable to all parties. "I don't want him here any more than you do," Max would say in his role of embattled ally subject to forces beyond his control. "We all have our crosses to bear." Or: "The two of you might like each other if you gave it a chance."

Unable to sleep, Terman would hear him in the early hours of the morning, typing in his room on the third floor at seemingly incredible speeds. The man left his room once or twice a day, at least when Terman was there to observe his behavior, to stretch his legs or to go to the bathroom. He seemed to take his meals in his room, though evidence for him eating anything at all was mostly circumstantial.

#

Terman thought he might rediscover the physical world through Tom's eyes—it was one of his secret justifications for sightseeing which he otherwise hated—but objects continued to evade him despite their insistent presence. He urged the visible world on his son, rushing him from place to place, hoping Tom would capture what his father missed. In his father's company, and out of it, Tom lacked the patience to obeserve. Sights went through him like a sieve, slipped away like unacknowledged feelings. They were there to witness each other's failure to witness.

One of the reasons he wrote fiction, he confided to Tom, was to account for exerience that otherwise eluded him.

"I know what you mean," Tom said. "It's like having a reminder of something you lived through." He thought of his thefts as a manifestation of the same principle, though at this point could barely recall the compulsion to steal.

"But the reminder is in code," Terman said, "and the code is impenetrable, so that the writing never reflects on the real life, if any, that inspired it. It invents its own experience."

"Which is to say it offers a substitute for real experience," Tom said. "You make it sound pretty dry."

"What the hell is real experience?"shouted Terman, arguing not with Tom but with private voices. "Fiction just exchanges one set of imagined possibilities for another."

#

Henry Berger, travelling with false passport, books two places on the next available flight to New York. He notices a small man with thick-lensed glasses watching him from behind a copy of Vogue. *Berger is reading a* News of the World *when the announcement comes that the plane is boarding. He stands up with the others, signals to the woman who is travelling with him, dawdles, lights a cigarette, hangs back at the end of the line. Why have an operative tail him? he wonders. Is it just a precaution on their part or are they aware of the full danger he represents to them? The woman standing next to him says, Why don't I turn in these tickets for something a little more convenient?*

#

Though Tom made no complaint, though he was dutiful in his admiration of whatever his father set before him to admire, he thought that they were doing things backwards, that this was what they ought to have done five weeks ago when he first arrived in London. It had taken all this time to get to first things, to provisional beginnings. He couldn't seem to remember why it had taken them so long to get started.

They were faced with a final decision, a last full day, and found themselves, brochures strewn across the parlor floor, paralyzed by a surfeit of choices. Upstairs, the fat man typed away, frightening in his decisiveness. The *mot juste,* several at once, Terman imagined, sprang to the page at his touch.

They replayed the same conversation they'd been having for the past two weeks, though appeared to switch roles. "You make the choice," Terman said.

"Yeah. Well, what if you don't like the choice I make?"

"Try me," said Terman, who already felt severely tried. Nothing they had done together, not one of the trips they had taken, had fully satisfied his expectations."

"I'll give you my reasoning first, okay?" Tom said, speaking quickly as if afraid the words might escape him if he hesitated even for a moment. "Obviously, there are any number of interesting places we haven't visited . Okay? Since we can't go to all of them, and since I have really no basis for choice, what I'd like to do instead is go to a film in the afternoon and say goodbye to Astrid in the evening, if that's all right with you, Dad."

What could he make of such soft treatment from his former enemy? "Why don't we sleep on it," Terman said, "and make a final decision in the morning? I think, insofar as we can make out what it is, we ought to do something memorable."

Tom looked at the movie listings in *Time Out* while Terman considered what his life would be like when Tom was gone. He had a book open on his lap but the words he read, or seemed to read, were only occasionally the ones that belonged to the text. He stopped himself and returned to the top of the page—the book was *Dom Casmurro* by Machado de Assis—determined to make connection with what appeared before his eyes. The words refused his attention. Although in English, they seemed to translate themselves into an unknown foreign tongue as he took them in.

It was almost midnight and the fat man was still typing in his room. He had stopped briefly at nine, then had started again a little after ten with renewed energy. "I'd like to kill him," Terman said. It was not what he planned to say. Tom looked up, startled. Terman laughed. "I don't mean everything I say," he said.

"I think you do," said Tom.

#

Terman had not seen it before, though he had been the principal writer under an assumed name, and so its rare appearance at the Electric Cinema (Tom had brought the movie to his attention) seemed almost providential. "I don't know if I can sit through it," Terman warned him, though the idea of going with his son to see something he had once collaborated on half appealed to him. The movie was called *Nightowl,* which was not its original title, which was the third or fourth title of the unhappy project. According to the note in *Time Out*, the movie had been discovered in a Worst Films Festival in San Francisco and had subsequently achieved something of a cult following. "The bizzare closure is one of the glories of the independent American Cinema."

The print, as it turned out, was bad, the colors faded. The theater seats were uncomfortable. A neon light flickered distractingly to the right of the screen. A handful of the small stunned audience staggererd out before the film's notable conclusion. Certain lines that he had particularly relished in the moment of creation were missing or significantly changed. Yet the event of the film moved him as if in looking at snapshots of children, he had come across a face he could not wholly account for but with which he shared recognizably some deeply buried secrets. His eyes teared mysteriously and he kept his hand at the side of his face to protect himself from embarrassment. He thought the direction self-conscious and static, though more accomplished than he had reason to expect. By focusing endlessly on the same few characters and objects, the camera forced the viewer, if he survived, to see them without preconception. The film had three false endings before the final unexpected one where the young boarder, the title figure, moves into the wife's bed in the guise of the husband he has just killed. "Close your eyes," he says to her in the other's voice before entering the bedroom. (And she does.) "I want you to remember me as I was." Her arms reach out in expectation to the approaching shadow.

Terman didn't ask him what he thought of it and Tom offered no response beyond an enthusiastic shaking of his head. "Yeah,"he said, an acknowledgement that they had watched this inexplicable movie together, that it was beyond them now, a part of the mutually experienced past. After the movie, he took Tom and Astrid to dinner at an overpriced seafood restaurant in Soho, then drove them both to Astrid's house. Disappointment that he wasn't invited in—he had been in top form throughout dinner and thought he rated more than thank you and goodnight—Terman went home alone. He didn't go right home but stopped off at Isabelle's apartment, parking just down the street. He sat in the car a few minutes, thinking of climbing out, entering the building, ringing the doorbell to her apartment, thinking of saying when she answered the door that he missed her terribly and wondered if they couldn't get together again (her answer, as he imagined it, was a mute refusal), then drove away, stripped of false hope. Each moment he seemed to get closer to himself.

#

The little man in the thick glasses is tied up, bound and gagged, and propped up in sitting position in one of the pay toilet booths. As Henry Berger leaves the Men's Room, he is passed by a middleaged Japanese man in a panama suit, the man glancing at him with more than casual interest. Walking briskly to another terminal, Berger boards a Pan Am flight to New York, the last passenger but one. Two attendants are getting ready to disconnect the ramp. "You're a lucky chap, aren't you?" one of them says to him. Someone else is coming. A moment later, the dark-haired woman he is travelling with also boards.

#

My father was in his study when I came in—it was like 2 AM—manuscript pages (I think that's what they were) spread out across the floor, his gun on his desk. I stuck my head in to say I was back, and that I thought I'd stay up the night and conk out, if I could, on the flight home.

"If you really want to do it, I'll stay up with you," he said.

He looked burnt out and his movements seemed barely coordinated. All the desk drawers were open, loose papers in five separate piles on the flöor, his waste basket flowing over. There was a stack of eight manuscript boxes alongside the desk. I watched for awhile without saying anything, trying to figure out what was going on.

"Do you think you'll ever see her again?" he asked.

I thought he was talking about my mother at first so I didn't understand what he meant, but he was referring to Astrid (or talking about himself and Isabelle). "You never know," I said.

"Did you make any arrangements with her?"

"Well, we exchanged addresses if that's what you mean. What are the boxes for, Dad?"

"Just cleaning up," he said. "I'll be through in a few minutes."

There was a tapping at the outside door, which my father ignored or seemed not to notice. It refused to go away, got louder, more persistent. I won't deny that it scared me.

"It sounds like he changed the keyboard of his typewriter," my father said, amused by the idea. "I like this tune better than the other."

#

When he heard the knocking on the door, Terman assumed the presumptuous fat man upstairs had gone out for an airing and had misplaced his key. "Don't answer it," Tom said. Terman was thinking the same thing, though after a few minutes he made his way to the door, not wanting to miss the opportunity for some new experience. The knocking, if that's what it was, had stopped. Terman saw a face in the window which startled him, yet renewed his faith in the possibilities for surprise in this life. He had the impression that the face belonged to Isabelle and he unlatched the door for her in a state of painful joy. "I'm glad you've come back," he said. The face belonged to Astrid, who had come to see Tom. She stood in the shadows, her manner a confusion of anger and abasement, waiting to be asked in. "Come on it," Terman said. He held out his hand.

Tom came down—he had been standing on the stairs while his father opened the door—and he and the girl talked in the parlor in soft halting voices. "I'm sorry if I woke anyone up?" Astrid said.

Terman was in his study sitting inertly in a chair, memorizing the recent past, the door closed against other voices. Nothing would ever escape him again, he decided. He resisted sleep so was taken by it unawares, was stolen from consciousness.

At some point Tom and the girl tiptoed up the stairs to the room on the second floor Tom had recently appropriated as his own. They were holding hands, as he and Isabelle had on occasion, or so Terman imagined them. It may have been they had their arms around each other and stopped on every second or third step to kiss.

Terman was thinking, as he slept or didn't, that someone ought to remind Tom to set the alarm on his clock.

In a hurry—he had to do it before he fell asleep—he walked in stocking feet down the long corridor to Tom's room. He slipped into the room, set the alarm for six thirty (Tom's flight left Heathrow at 8:20), barely glancing at the entangled couple. He imagined himself closing the door behind him as he left the room.

#

After his plane lands at JFK, after he and his companion (who may or may not be his wife) clear customs, Henry Berger goes into a public phone booth and dials a long distance number from memory. "I'm coming in," he says without identifying himself. "Henry," says the other, "where are you, boy? We've been expecting you posthaste."

"I'll be there before you know it," Berger says. "Leave a light burning in the window for me, will you?"

"Do you want us to bring you in from the airport? Might be the most effective procedure."

"I'd prefer making an unannounced entrance," Berger says. "And I want the President in the room when we talk."

"He understands that."

After Henry Berger leaves the phone booth, he takes his companion to a taxi, a gentlemanly excess perhaps not in his best interests. "See you in a couple of days," he says through the two inch opening in the window. He takes a cab himself to LaGuardia Airport and catches the Washington shuttle, which is already boarding as he arrives.

#

The story moves abruptly toward its conclusion, though I confuse in the telling beginnings and ends.

I couldn't seem to get out of the house, kept leaving things behind or losing them. After all the false starts, we drove to the airport in a white heat, my father silent for the duration of the ride, his manner like a reprimand. I asked him if something was wrong and he said if he thought about it long enough he would probably find something. We queued up to check the larger of my two bags, getting at first on the wrong line, investing at least ten minutes in misplaced expectation. After some frantic rushing about, we were told that the departure time of my flight had been delayed forty-five minutes, and we stopped at an overcrowded cafeteria for some breakfast. We had just gotten our food to an unoccupied table when the loudspeaker announced that TWA Flight 144, which was mine, was boarding at some unintelligible gate and we were up again, rushing to no purpose. I bought some chewing gum, an *International Herald Tribune,* and a copy of E. M. Forster's *The Longest Journey*, my father choosing the book and paying the bill. A flashbulb went off. Someone took our picture or the picture of some people standing directly behind us, the lights blinding me momentarily. There was a point beyond which only passengers were allowed and we said goodbye and then embraced. "Keep in touch, Tom," he said. I said I would do my best. There didn't seem time for anything else.

They frisked me at the security checkout and for a dislocated moment I thought I still had my father's pistol in my pocket and would have to answer for the theft. The frisking was only a formality—something in my manner, my style maybe, offended them—a last gesture of English hospitality. Then I was on the plane, seated at a window toward the front of the No Smoking section. Not many of the people around me looked like they were going to America and I had that moment of panic (I've had it before on other flights) when you think you've gotten on the wrong plane or that the plane you're on has some telling defect that only you have discovered. I thought of making some excuse and getting out. There was time for that, time for everything. The plane sat for another hour and ten minutes and I thought, Well, we're not going anywhere. The plane I'm on is committed to staying in place. I took a stick of gum and offered the pack to the woman in the business suit next to me. "It's just what I need," she said.

#

It could not be said that he hadn't felt anything. What didn't he feel? An obscure free-floating ache accompanied him on the return from Heathrow, the skin of his face stretched tight against the bones, his eyes, despite sunglasses, troubled by the muted English light. There were a number of things he had to do and he concentrated on the sequence of the doing, his consciousness a scratch list of notes to himself. Take in the milk. Open mail. Account his feelings. Wash the dishes in the sink and put them away. Finish packing manuscripts. Settle accounts. Make all the beds. Go to the post office. Settle accounts.

The intruder's room, which was unlocked and temporarily unoccupied, smelled of some deodorizing substance, a sweet treacly odor with a dank subtext. Terman sat at the table the fat man presumably used as a desk and stared at his reflection which glowered back, no comradship there, narrow-eyed and hard. He made disdainful faces at the opposing face and was responded to in kind. Whatever the fat man had been working on was apparently locked away in the attaché case on the bed or had gone with him. Only a few blank sheets of bond occupied the work table. There was nothing Terman wanted from the intruder beyond the absence of his intrusion and even that prospect offered no long-lived pleasure. He went through the wastebasket and caught the name Henry Berger on a discarded sheet of manuscript. "I can't take you with me, sweetheart," he was saying to an unidentified woman. The woman said: "I can make a terrible enemy when left to my own devices."

After heaving the attaché case through an open window, Terman went to his own study and completed the packing of manuscrupts he had started the evening before. A rhythm established itself, an odd metronomic music that was sometimes indistinguishable from the beat of his heart. When he was done he addressed the packages to his American agent, wrote two long overdue letters, loaded the car and drove to the post office.

He left the car where he had parked it near the post office and walked back to the house he no longer thought of as his special province. His son was gone—that registered for the first time in a while. Some weeks ago—it might have been yesterday—he had been anticipating the visit (not altogether happily, let it be admitted), and now it was over. He was whistling or the man that wore his clothes and walked in his shoes and animated his bones was whistling. His behavior seemed inexplicable even to himself.

On his walking in the door—the house was less familiar with each revisit—he remembered typing the last line of his first novel and then floating from his chair more in relief than triumph, emptied of everything, the satisfaction as sharp as a toothache in the night. The recollection came and went, taking away more than it had brought. What was done was irrevocably done. He would never know again, except as memory allowed, what it was like to complete the last line of that first book. The memory of it only made him more aware of the real thing that was lost to him. No pleasure had been so intense in his life, or so he imagined, as the completion of that first book. He fastened on the notion of loss and the arbitrariness of memory. The aging process rode roughshod over everything, leaving dust and decay in its wake.

This section of his life was done with, he told himself, as if he were referring to a piece of writing, a novel or a screenplay. It was time to move on, he thought, to find another space in which to move, the language without specific reference. He put his typewriter into its faded blue case and closed the cover.

Each succeeding move invented itself. He phoned Isabelle and caught her, as she said, on the way out. "I've called to say goodbye," he said. She didn't ask where he was going, goodbye to what? "You're all right, are you?" she asked. He felt, he said, at the top of his game. "Goodbye, sweetheart," he said.

"Sweetheart, is it? Yes, I'm sure. Is there anything else you wanted to say before I hang up on you. I do have to go in minute."

The minute passed. He said goodbye a second time. She said, "Speak to you anon," and was gone. (Later, on the way to work, or on the way home, she might wonder at the implication of his call.)

The desk was all but clear. He thought of polishing it, but settled for dusting it rigorously with an old sock. The gun, which occupied a central place, had to be moved and removed, shifted from place to place like an unwanted child. The dusting completed, he lifted the pistol from the desk and balanced it in his palm. It was loaded for use—the whole point of a gun was its function—or had he only imagined himself loading it? He checked and double checked. What he wanted to say to Isabelle was that he could still remember having cared for her, though the feeling, which ebbed a little each day, was disappearing. For a moment, he felt an extraordinary tenderness for the few remaining objects in the room: couch, desk, desk chair, manuscript boxes, false starts on balls of paper in the waste basket. He held the gun to the side of his head.

Everything was in order or—there was that alternative—the disorder was in itself complete. Still, he might have missed something, forgotten some crucial detail, left something undone thinking it done. Had he made the beds? Had he accounted his feelings at the moment he raised the pistol to his head. At the moment after that. At the one after that. At *this* moment? The next step, the step that followed the step before it, that step following on the heels of its predecessor, was to.... The sentence, suspended in possibility, moved inexorably toward a resolution it would never achieve.

#

He is sure that no one has followed him on the last lap of his journey and almost equally certain that no one knows he is in Washington, D.C. He has written nothing down, has confided in no one. The evidence, the full burden of his discovery, is lodged in his head. He hails a cab but instead of going directly to the White House, he stops off at the Phillips Museum. He calls his contact from a museum phone and says, "Expect me at exactly five minutes after one." "I'll leave word at the desk that you're to be sent up on the President's elevator," the friend says. "What name are you using?" "Lukas Terman," says Berger.

He goes through the museum, moving intently from painting to painting, as though he might carry with him the memory of so much extraordinary work. The camera scans the paintings, as Henry Berger might, its eye crossing the walls like a beam of light.

When he leaves the museum he gets into another cab and instructs the driver (or so we imagine)—we perceive the conversation from outside the cab, from the distance of a bystander—to take him to the White House. We follow the taxi through the streets of Washington, Berger's eyes closing and opening, tiredness catching up.

We pick up Henry Berger as he leaves the cab and walks tentatively up the White house steps, the sun, glancing off the facade, blinding him. Among the crowd of tourists, there is no one he knows. A fat man, camera around his neck, wearing a sky blue shirt with a flame of ghastly orange flamingos across its front, seems to want to ask Berger something, steps awkwardly in his way. "Yes?" "Got the time?" asks the pilgrim. Berger, smiling, a tourist himself at this moment, lifts his left arm to glance at his watch. "Five after one," he says, or starts to say, one hand eclipsing the other. There is a gunshot from the camera or from somewhere above and beyond the camera. A carnation of blood appears at Berger's chest. Someone cheers or jeers. The detective's face register's all, amazement, the cancellation of hope, the death of passion, disillusion beyond further disillusion. The camera catches him in freeze frame as he falls backwards, the steps moving under his feet, his arms out anticipating momentary flight.

#

The 747 taxis down a runway, changes direction, stops and starts, trapped in indecision. And then without further announcement, just when I think we'll never go anywhere, we tear loose from the earth, ascend with heartbreaking abruptness.

I remember this time when I was a kid of eight or nine and I was eating breakfast by myself in the kitchen (corn flakes with half-thawed frozen raspberries) and the doorbell rang and we weren't expecting anyone and I answered (my mother out shopping, Kate playing solitaire in her room) and my father was there and he lifted me onto his shoulders and I asked him if he had come to stay and he mumbled something which I took to be yes and for that moment before I heard in echo what he actually said I had this sense that everything was all right not only that but it was going to be all right for a long time to come and until I realized that I had misheard his answer I was so glad so glad I mean I can't even remember the feeling only that it rang in my head like a siren or a scream and I didn't want to give it up (I was flying on his shoulders) and when it was gone it was gone.

FICTION COLLECTIVE

Books in Print

	Price List: cloth	paper
The Second Story Man by Mimi Albert	8.95	3.95
Althea by J.M. Alonso	11.95	4.95
Searching for Survivors by Russell Banks	7.95	3.95
Babble by Jonathan Baumbach	8.95	3.95
Chez Charlotte and Emily by Jonathan Baumbach	9.95	4.95
My Father More or Less by Jonathan Baumbach	11.95	5.95
Reruns by Jonathan Baumbach	7.95	3.95
Things in Place by Jerry Bumpus	8.95	3.95
Ø Null Set by George Chambers	8.95	3.95
The Winnebago Mysteries by Moira Crone	10.95	4.95
Amateur People by Andrée Connors	8.95	3.95
Take It or Leave It by Raymond Federman	11.95	4.95
Coming Close by B.H. Friedman	11.95	5.95
Museum by B.H. Friedman	7.95	3.95
Temporary Sanity by Thomas Glynn	8.95	3.95
The Talking Room by Marianne Hauser	8.95	3.95
Holy Smoke by Fanny Howe	8.95	3.95
Mole's Pity by Harold Jaffe	8.95	3.95
Mourning Crazy Horse by Harold Jaffe	11.95	5.95
Moving Parts by Steve Katz	8.95	3.95
Find Him! by Elaine Kraf	9.95	3.95
Emergency Exit by Clarence Major	9.95	4.95
Reflex and Bone Structure by Clarence Major	8.95	3.95
Four Roses in Three Acts by Franklin Mason	9.95	4.95
The Secret Table by Mark Mirsky	7.95	3.95
Encores for a Dilettante by Ursule Molinaro	8.95	3.95
Rope Dances by David Porush	8.95	3.95
The Broad Back of the Angel by Leon Rooke	9.95	3.95
The Common Wilderness by Michael Seide	16.95	--
The Comatose Kids by Seymour Simckes	8.95	3.95
Fat People by Carol Sturm Smith	8.95	3.95
The Hermetic Whore by Peter Spielberg	8.95	3.95
Twiddledum Twaddledum by Peter Spielberg	7.95	3.95
Long Talking Bad Conditions Blues by Ronald Sukenick	9.95	4.95
98.6 by Ronald Sukenick	7.95	3.95
Meningitis by Yuriy Tarnawsky	8.95	3.95
Heretical Songs by Curtis White	9.95	4.95
Statements 1	--	3.95
Statements 2	8.95	2.95